Amos Tutuola was born in Abeokuta, Nigeria, in 1920. The son of a cocoa farmer, he attended several schools before training as a blacksmith. He later worked as a civil servant. His first novel, *The Palm-Wine Drinkard*, was published in 1952 and brought him international recognition. From 1956 until retirement, he worked for the Nigerian Broadcasting Company while continuing to write. His last book, *The Village Witch Doctor and Other Stories*, was published in 1990. He died in Ibadan in 1997.

by the same author

THE PALM-WINE DRINKARD
MY LIFE IN THE BUSH OF GHOSTS
SIMBI AND THE SATYR OF THE DARK JUNGLE
FEATHER WOMAN OF THE JUNGLE
AJAIYI AND HIS INHERITED POVERTY
THE WITCH-HERBALIST OF THE REMOTE TOWN
PAUPER, BRAWLER AND SLANDERER
THE VILLAGE WITCH DOCTOR AND OTHER STORIES

The Brave African Huntress

AMOS TUTUOLA

FABER & FABER

First published in 1958
by Faber & Faber Limited
Bloomsbury House, 74–77 Great Russell Street
London WC1B 3DA
This paperback edition first published in 2014

Typeset by Faber & Faber Limited
Printed and bound by CPI Group (UK) Ltd, Croydon, CR0 4YY

A CIP record for this book is available from the British Library

ISBN: 978-0-571-31689-2

Contents

The Brave African Huntress   1

But What About the Jungle of the Pigmies?   3

Why I Inherited my Father's Hunting
     Profession   6

The Day that I Inherit my Father's Hunting
     Profession   11

Accidental Occurrence on the Way to the
     Jungle of the Pigmies   14

How I Fought with "Odara" and Conquered
     Him in the Semi-jungle   16

In the Ibembe Town   26

I Became the Private Barber for the King of
     Ibembe Town   37

Please, Lay Your Head on this Rock and Let
     me cut it off at Once!   45

In the Jungle of the Pigmies   54

The Animal that Died but his Eyes still Alive   66

The Huge Stern Pigmy Captured Me   73

My Life in the Town of the Pigmies—the Town
    Under the Rock   83

The Hard Life of the Custody   88

The Huntress is back to the Town and the
    Pigmies are in Danger   100

The Kind Gorilla Saved Me from the Debris   105

From the Jungle to the Bachelors' Town   114

In the Bachelors' Town   121

The Rolling and Talking Guord   143

Back to the Jungle of the Pigmies   148

Good-bye to the Jungle of the Pigmies   164

The Brave African Huntress

I Adebisi, the African huntress, will first relate the adventure of my late father, one of the ancient brave hunters, in brief:

My father was a brave hunter in his town. He had hunted in several dangerous jungles which the rest hunters had rejected to enter or even to approach because of fear of being killed by the wild animals and harmful creatures of the jungle.

My father had killed thousands of the wild animals and wonderful animals which were no more seen or which were not known to us nowadays. And he had fought and conquered uncountable curious creatures as—elves, genii, goblins, demons, imps, gnomes, etc., whose homes were in these jungles.

He had plenty of super-natural powers and his gods were countless. All these gods were occupied a half part of his house. They were always making fearful noises in both day and night in both house and in the compound. In respect of the fearful attitudes of his gods, his friends and neighbours who were not brave enough could not enter his house whenever he went to hunt in the jungle.

Whenever my father was preparing to go and hunt

in the jungle, before he would go he would first make several kinds of sacrifices. He would kill many goats for his gods, he would sacrifice a large number of cocks and plenty of palm oil to the witches—those old and weary mothers who were sleeping always in the dark rooms—the windowless and unventilated rooms which surrounded the compound. These old and weary mothers were so old and weary that they never attempted to come out from the rooms more than ten years ago. They were also protecting my father from the wild animals, etc., etc. And countless dogs would be sacrificed to the god of iron the very day that he would leave for the jungle.

But What About the Jungle of the Pigmies?

But there was still one jungle which was called—The Jungle of the Pigmies. This jungle was the most dreadful of all the jungles which were not so far from the town. The Jungle of the Pigmies was at a distance of about one hundred miles from the town. It was in this jungle the pigmies who were supposed to be the owners of it were living. The jungle was the home of all the wild animals and the most harmful creatures which were not found in the rest jungles. There the home of the wonderful birds which had the voices similar to that of the human being. There the home of the head of all snakes—the boa constrictor.

Thousands of hunters from the different parts of the towns who had gone to hunt in this jungle never returned. Once a person entered this jungle would not be seen again.

There were so many kinds of fruit-trees which the people preferred to eat always. And under the ground of this jungle, there were metals as brass, copper, etc., with which the people were making trays, bowls, gods, idols. They were also making the cutlasses, knives, hoes, etc., from the iron which were dug out from there. All these things were attracting the people to force themselves to go there as well.

My father had four sons before I was born, but one day, when they went to this jungle to fetch for one of the metals, they were not seen again. Whether they were killed by the wild animals, etc., or they were detained by the pigmies nobody could say, but this was a great sorrow to my father.

As a great number of the people were perishing in this jungle every year, then the people of about fifty towns made a meeting between themselves to go there and kill all the wild animals, etc., and all the pigmies. They thought that if they did so perhaps there would be no more fear and the people or hunters might be able to go there as they liked. And they went there as they resolved but the pigmies drove them away and thousands of them were taken as prisoners by the pigmies. So as from that day there was no one of them who attempted to go near this jungle again. Of course all hunters believed that the pigmies were living in there but they did not know the real part of it in which they were living.

As the only four sons whom my father had, had perished or were detained by the pigmies. Therefore, his ambition was always to go and hunt in this dreadful jungle, after the rest hunters had already shunned there, perhaps he might be able to find out his four sons.

So one day, he invited all the hunters to his house. He told them that he was going to the Jungle of the Pigmies. But it was a great surprise and fear to those hunters to hear like that from my father. They advised him not to go back to this jungle but he did not follow their advice at all.

After several days travel with much difficulties he reached this jungle. He killed many wild animals, he fought with many other harmful creatures and he conquered them. But when uncountable pigmies attacked him and they did not allow him to travel as far as he wished in this jungle perhaps he might come across his sons, then he took some of the animals which he killed and he returned to the town. But it was a great surprise to the people of the town to see him returned safely. As from that time he was going to hunt in this jungle regularly. But he was still in great sorrow because as he was going there he did not see any trace of his sons at all. At last when he became old he stopped to go and hunt in this jungle again. Then all the hunters of the town and from the various towns installed him the head of hunters, because he was only the hunter who was brave enough to hunt in the Jungle of the Pigmies.

Why I Inherited my Father's Hunting Profession

I was eight years old when my father retired from his hunting profession. After he had retired, he leaned his "shakabullah" gun on his god of iron. He hung his hunting bag, cutlass, his wearing super-natural powers and all his hunting dresses before his god of iron as well. Then he invited all the hunters and a big ceremony was performed. So since that day he became a farmer. He was planting his food as yam, cassava, corn, pepper, etc. But as he was the head of all the hunters who were always coming to his house for advices about the wild animals, dangerous creatures, etc. So whenever those hunters were coming to his house, they were coming there with many smoked small animals which they killed in the jungle and they would give them to him as presents and thus they were giving him the animals every day.

He loved me so much that he did not like me to go far from him at any moment because he had no other daughter or son.

As I was then eight years of age, so I could decide within myself anything that a person might tell me in the indirect way. For the help of this, so one day, as I was playing about in the town and when a woman who sat at the front of her house saw me, she did not know the time that she said loudly—"Oh, sorry, if Adebisi's four brothers had not died in the Jungle of the Pigmies, one of them would inherit or take over now their father's hunting profession which will soon die away from their generation!"

When I overheard like that from this woman, I stopped to play along with the other children but I ran back home with sorrow. Although before I overheard like that from this woman, I had seen several clothes in my father's room which were blonged to young men. But whenever I asked from my father that who were the owners of these clothes, he would sighed greatly instead to tell me that the clothes were blonged to my brothers, his four sons, who had gone to the Jungle of the Pigmies and not returned.

When I overheard from this woman and when I ran back home, I sat closely to my father. Then I was thinking seriously in my mind whether my father had had another sons before I was born. But when my father and mother noticed that I sat down and became serious unexpectedly, they asked from me that what was wrong with me, but I replied that there was nothing wrong with me, I did not tell them the fact.

One day, when the fresh corn and yam were just out, I followed my father to his farm. When it was about twelve o'clock, when the half-day's work was ended, he roasted plenty of fresh corn and yams. As we were eating them, I asked from him whether he had had four sons before I was born because a few days ago I overheard from a woman said so.

When my father heard like that from me he groaned for a few minutes and then he explained to me that he had had four sons before I was born but all of them had gone to the Jungle of the Pigmies and not returned since then. He said further that he could not say definitely whether they were killed by the wild animals of that jungle or they were in the custody of the pigmies.

After my father had explained to me like that and I confirmed that it was true I had had four senior brothers before. So I told him at the same time that when I grew old enough I would go to that jungle to fight the pigmies until I would see that I conquered them and then I would bring my four brothers back to you if they were still alive.

But when my father heard like that from me he laughed greatly for a few minutes. After that he said—"Even a brave huntsman could not travel as far as he wished in this jungle before the wild animals or a number of the pigmies would kill him how much more for a young lady like you (myself) who could not even reach the jungle before the wild animals will kill her without any trouble!" When my father explained to me like that with laugh, I told him again that I would first kill all of the wild animals before I would start to find where the pigmies were living in the jungle. I told him as well that before I would attempt to go to the jungle I would see that I had already become a good huntress, and I would inherit his hunting profession. But my father did not believe me when I promised to do so.

Instead he explained further that there was in this jungle, a kind of a wonderful animal which he had never come across since when he had been hunting. He told me that this wonderful animal had about sixteen horns on forehead. Each of the horns was about six feet long and very thick, and sharp at the end. All these horns were faced its front accurately. He said that this animal had a kind of two fearful eyes which had a kind of powerful light. The ray of the light was round and was moving along with this animal as it was going along. The light of the eyes never quenched at any time but it (light) could not travel far. He told me further that there was a kind of a boa constrictor which was so fearful and powerful that he never attempted once to shoot it till he stopped hunting. And he told me as well about several kinds of creatures which were made this jungle more dangerous.

As I had heard the full story of my four brothers from my father so I did not fear at all to go to this jungle. So after a few days, I started to practise hunting. I was setting ropes in the bush for small animals. When I was perfect in that, then I started to stone at birds and squirrels which were in a far distance or on high trees. After I became perfect in that again, I bought a very small gun. This gun was so light that I was easily carrying it about with me. In a few years time I became perfect in shooting. After that I started to learn all the characteristics of the wild animals and about other harmful creatures.

When I became perfect in all these things and when I became fifteen years old. One day, I told my father frankly that I wanted to go and hunt in the Jungle of the Pigmies. But he was first greatly shocked immediately he heard like that from me and at the same moment he said loudly—"Oh, no wonder that you have started to practise hunting since when you were eight years of age!" and he did not tell me whether to go or not. But a few days later, I told him again about this jungle but yet he rejected my request after he had explained to me that as I was a lady therefore I could not go and hunt in either bush or forest or jungle. He said further that the hunting profession blonged to men only.

But when I became eighteen years of age, and when he noticed that I was not as happy as before I began to tell him to allow me to go to the jungle, then he agreed. But he told me that before I would go, I must first inherit the hunting profession from him. He explained that the day I would inherit the profession there would be a great ceremony. All hunters and the people of the town would be invited to the ceremony. When he agreed to my request I was so happy that I told him at the same time that I would go to the jungle in five days' time.

The Day that I Inherit my Father's Hunting Profession

The son of thief inherits "thieving".
The son of poor man inherits "poverty".
The son of lazy man inherits "laziness".
The son of rich man inherits "wealth".
The son of philosopher inherits "philosophy".
The son of hunter inherits "gun, etc."
so the "poverty", "misery", "wretchedness", and
"sorrow" shall never finish in the generation
that there is no "perseverance".

Therefore, I was going to inherit my father's hunting profession, although I was a lady. Before that day was reached my father had made the necessary arrangement. And it was hardly early in the morning of the day that I was leaving for the Jungle of the Pigmies, when several thousands of hunters with their "shaka-bullah" guns came to my father's house in respect of the "inheritance" of his hunting profession and in respect of my leaving for the jungle that day and almost all the people of the town came to my father's house as well just to witness this ceremony. Everyone was supplied with food and all kinds of drinks as well.

When it was one o'clock p.m. prompt, and after the whole of those hunters, etc., had eaten and drunken to their entire satisfaction, then my father presented his hunting dress, hunting-bag, cutlass, "shakabullah" gun, jujus, gods, etc., to me and I knelt down and took them from him. After that I wore the hunting dress, I put the gun and the hunting-bag on my left shoulder, I put the big native cap on head, and I put the jujus on my waist and fingers. After I did all these things I knelt down before those hunters. As they were praying for me that—"Though you are a lady and you are still young to go and hunt in the Jungle of the Pigmies, but as you are going there or volunteer your life to go there for the benefit of this town and others, however you come across difficulties in the jungle, you will come back to us as your father had done!" those people who were not hunters, my mother, sisters, friends, etc., were weeping bitterly. All were telling me not to attempt to go and hunt in this jungle, because they thought that I would not be able to return. But I did not listen to them, because I had become wild at the same moment that I had put on the hunting dress and jujus.

Having prayed before my father's gods—"to help me to return safely" then I first shot my gun into the sky just to show the crowd that I was ready to leave. After that I stood in attention in the centre of the crowd and I announced loudly with sharp and fearless voice—"Now, old women, old men, young men and children, I am leaving you all this afternoon for the Jungle of the Pigmies! Though I am young and I am a lady but for the benefit of our town and many others, I shall go there and I shall see that I kill or drive the whole pigmies away from that jungle and I shall see that I kill the whole wild and wonderful animals of that jungle before I will come to you or to die in the jungle if I cannot bring back those hunters, etc., who were in the custody of the pigmies for a long time. So, I thank you all for the warm affection you have on me. I pray to God to let us meet again. Good-bye to you all! good-bye!"

Immediately I bade them "good-bye" and they too did so with great sorrow, then I started to go to the jungle. As I was going along the whole people were following me and the hunters were shooting their guns repeatedly. The people who were not hunters were telling me loudly—"Come back, don't go to the Jungle of the Pigmies, it is a bad jungle!" but I did not listen to them, I was just going on as hastily as I could. The whole of the crowd, my father, mother, sisters and friends followed me until I left the town before they went back from me with their hands which were waving to me with sorrow until I was vanished to their view.

It was like that I left my town and my people and started to go to this jungle.

It was the "Day of New Creation" which was Thursday, that I left my town for this jungle.

Accidental Occurrence on the Way to the Jungle of the Pigmies

After the crowd had gone back from me and as the "snail never leave his shell behind whenever he is going on journey". Therefore I stopped on the roadside I took out all the jujus which were inside the hunting bag, just to make sure whether they were there. But it was a great pity that the "drunkard had forgotten poverty". I had forgotten the most important of all my jujus at home. I did not remember to take it back after the sacrifice had given to it. And I forgot that I would need the help of it throughout my journey.

Anyhow, I continued to travel along as hastily as I could so that I might be travelled very far away before the nightfall. Although this jungle was about one hundred miles away from my town. But when I travelled up to ten miles and when the darkness of the nightfall did not allow me to see well then I stopped. I made the fire under a small tree which was at the roadside. I roasted one small yam and I ate it, after that I slept without fear of any danger of the night, because that day was the "Day of New Creation" which was Thursday.

Very early in the morning, I woke up, I did not wait to eat anything but I continued to travel along at once.

But when I travelled for two hours on this road, I came to where several roads crossed themselves. This was the junction of roads that which used to confuse the stranger, because I did not know which of these roads to travel to the jungle. Then I stopped there and I was thinking in mind how to distinguish the right one which led to the jungle. I was so sad as the rat which was sent to the cat, when I was forced to stop there by this junction. At last when I did not know which was the right one that led to the jungle, I slept there till following morning which was "The Day of three Resolutions" Saturday.

But when it was morning, I took my gun, hunting bag, and cutlass and then I simply took one of these roads, I was travelling along as quickly as possible. To my fear when I travelled for about four hours on this road I travelled to the end of it. There was no real road on which to travel again. But instead to stop I started to travel along in the forest, and when it was three o'clock p.m., I entered a small semi-jungle as I could call it because it was not a real jungle.

How I Fought with "Odara" and Conquered Him in the Semi-jungle

The heavy rain that stops the voices of birds.

After I travelled in this semi-jungle for a few minutes, I started to look for birds to shoot to death for my food, but it was a surprise to me when I did not see anything like a bird in this semi-jungle at all. Anyhow I stopped, I made fire and I roasted a yam and I ate it. After I ate the roasted yam and I was just thinking within myself where to get water to drink, there I saw at that moment, about six hunters appeared from the different direction of this semi-jungle. They asked me that from which town did I come to hunt in that jungle and I told them the name of my town. And I too asked from them the name of their town, they told me the name of their town as well and they said that it was not far from that jungle. But when I told them that it was not in this semi-jungle I came to hunt in particular, but I was going to hunt in the Jungle of the Pigmies, they were nearly shocked to death at the same moment.

They shook up and down their heads with great

fear when they thought over about the cruel creatures, wild animals and pigmies of the jungle. They warned me seriously not to go there but I insisted to go. As I noticed that they were hungry, I gave them one of my yams and they roasted it and ate it at once. Then after we chatted for a few minutes I told them that I was thirsty and as they too were thirsty, they told me to stand up and follow them to a small river which was not so far from that place. As I was following them to the river, they were telling me that I should be talking to them very softly because if "Odara" the giant-like or cyclops-like creature as I could describe him and who was the owner of this semi-jungle, heard my voice or any one else, would come out and kill us. They told me that there was no another creature who lived in that jungle with him except animals. Because "Odara" was too harsh, cruel, greedily, etc. As these hunters were still telling me the story of "Odara" as we were going along to the river, there we were hearing faintly, the noises which were coming from a long distance. The noises were just as if thousands of hooligans were following their cruel and merciless leader to some place where they were going to cause harm to several people. Then these hunters who had already known the attitudes of "Odara" listened to the noises as we were still going along.

A few minutes more, these noises were approaching us nearer and thus the noises were approaching us more and more until the hunters were quite sure that "Odara" and his followers were coming to that direction. As they were telling me that everyone of us must find somewhere to hide himself or herself, the followers of "Odara", who were at a little distance from their leader, "Odara" were then seeing and coming to that direction. Then unexpectedly and without telling one another where to hide, we scattered into the jungle. Many of us crept into the refuses, some hid inside the large holes and some climbed the hill and hid on top of it but I climbed to the top of a big tree and I hid myself on top of it. This tree was not far from the road so that I might see "Odara" and his followers clearly when they were passing along through that place. The leaves of the tree on which I hid were so covered me that if I did not climb this tree on presence of somebody there was nobody who could believe that I was there. Then everyone of us kept as quiet in his or her hiding place and stopped talking as when the heavy rain stopped the voices of birds.

We hardly hid ourselves when the followers of "Odara" were passing through that direction.

"Odara's" followers were more than fifty in number and each of them held harmful weapons. They were hastily looking at the tops and at the bottoms of the trees and hills as well. They were shouting greatly with fearful voices.

But when I peeped through the leaves, I saw them clearly that they did not wear jacket or to cover their bodies with any cloth or to put on their heads anything like caps but they wore only very short trousers. These trousers were so red that everyone of these followers could be easily seen from a long distance. Everyone of them put on the ears big round rings. As they were going along as hastily as they could it was so they were looking at back always just to see whether their leader, "Odara" was approaching nearer.

As they were going along it was so they were shouting greatly —"Let all the animals of this semi-jungle leave this road for another place, because 'Odara' the possessor of the poisonous cudgels, is coming behind! Let the snakes and birds of this jungle leave the road, the possessor of the poisonous cudgels, 'Odara' is coming behind!" thus these "Odara's" followers were warning every creature to leave the road for "Odara" as they were going along.

When I heard this announcement I feared greatly and I did not shake my body at that moment so that they might not see me and thus the other hunters did as well. But after a few minutes that "Odara's" followers had gone, and as I was about to rub away all the stinging ants which were stinging me repeatedly, there I saw unexpectedly that more than one thousand bush animals, birds, snakes, etc., were running as hastily as they could with closed eyes to every direction of this jungle. They were hiding themselves inside the holes, under the refuses, etc., and the snakes and birds were hiding on top of trees. As I was still wondering when I saw them that they were doing like that, a very strong wind came. This wind was so strong that the whole jungle was in disorder at the same moment. This wind was blowing to the trees so heavily that their tops or branches were touching the ground and all the dried leaves and refuses were blown to the great height in the sky, so these signs showed me that "Odara" was approaching.

As I was still wondering about these curious signs and the ants were still stinging every part of my body so painfully that I could no longer afford it to remain on top of that tree except to come down and as I was just preparing to come down. There I heard a great fearful shout of "Odara". He was then at a distance of about one-cighth of a mile. When I heard this again I did not attempt to come down as I thought to do but I simply gave my body to these stinging ants. When "Odara" came nearer all the hills and trees were shaking, his voice was hearing all over the jungle. When he travelled near the tree on top of which I hid, he stopped because he suspected that someone was on top of it. He raised his big head up and he gazed at the top of this tree. And as he was still shouting greatly I saw him clearly. He was too terrible indeed to be seen for a human being, and I feared him so much that I did not know when I opened my mouth and the spit was dropping down. He hung a large bag on left shoulder in which plenty of the "poisonous cudgels" were kept and he held a bunch of the same kind of the cudgels with left hand as well.

"Odara" seemed as the jungle giant. He was very tall and stout. He had a very rough body and this body was full of knots and his face was full of big pimples and his body was full of scars. His head was just as a small round hill, the hairs of his body were very long and rough in such a way that they could not be distinguished from the refuses. He wore a huge thick and dirty trousers which could only reach his knees. Big and small cowries were tied to every part of the trousers in such a perfect way that the trousers itself could not be seen at all except those cowries. The cowries were full of the rotten blood and feathers of birds were stuck to the rotten blood. His eyes were so big and fearful that I was unable to look at them more than once.

As he gazed at the top of the tree on which I hid and as I was still looking at his fearful appearances he shouted greatly unexpectedly with terrible voice just to make sure whether there was somebody who hid on top of that tree. But when the other hunters and I heard his shout unexpectedly, we did not know the time when we shook our bodies with great fear and this showed "Odara" that we hid there. But as he saw me when I shook and as he was coming to that tree. I thought what I could do to safe myself from him and I remembered at the same moment to shoot my gun to him perhaps he would die. Then without hesitation, I shot my "shakabullah" gun to him. But to my great fear was that before my "shakabullah" gun sounded—"Shaka—bul—laha!" this wonderful creature, "Odara" the possessor of the poisonous cudgels, or the jungle giant, had caught the gun-shots with right hand and he swallowed them at the same time and I feared greatly that the gun-shots did not hurt his palm at all. Now he became more angry than ever because I shot him. And immediately he had swallowed the gun-shots he started to throw several poisonous cudgels to the top of that tree. As he was still throwing several cudgels to the top of that tree so that I might fall down and then to kill me, it was so many poisonous snakes were climbing that tree from the bottom so that they might hide themselves on top of it when they heard the fearful shout of "Odara" and this was another great fear to me as well. When they climbed the tree to where I hid they were biting at my legs and ankles so that I might give them chance to hide in there and I was very lucky that the poisons of their teeth did not harm me but they were falling back to the ground and they were dying at once instead because my ankles had already injected with a kind of medicine before I left my town.

When "Odara" saw that I did not come down as he was throwing his cudgels to me repeatedly, the cudgels which were so poisonous that immediately they touched a living creature or a person would die at once. So he came nearer to the tree, he began to shake it with all his powers so that I might fall down. But as he was doing so he smashed Ojo, one of those hunters, who hid near this tree and with pain Ojo did not know when he stood up just to run away for his life, and at the same moment "Odara" snatched him. He first slapped him at belly before he threw him inside the huge bag which he hung on shoulder. After that he continued to shake the tree and again with great fear I shot my "shakabullah" gun to him for the second time. But to my fear again was that before my gun sounded—"Shaka—bul—laha!" "Odara" had caught the gun-shots with his left hand and at the same moment he swallowed them.

When he did so again and when I believed that my "shakabullah" gun could not do anything to him, I feared him so much that I did not know the time that I fell from the top of that tree to the ground without my wish and I hardly reached the ground when I jumped up and began to run away for my life and he was chasing me along to catch.

As I was running away I ran to the part of the jungle in which the rest hunters hid themselves all the while. When they heard as I was shouting greatly for help along to the spot that they hid they thought that "Odara" had seen them as well and he was coming to kill them. For this reason the whole of them came out from their hiding places at a time. They started to run away for their lives at once. But immediately "Odara" saw them as well, he started to stagger about, and as he was chasing this and that he left to chase me unnoticed, because he wanted to catch the whole of us at a time. He had forgotten that a person who chased two rats at a time would lose all. Then at the same moment I was running furiously along to where I would be saved. But unfortunately it was this time my hunting bag which was on my shoulder all the while, was hooked by big thorns of a mighty tree while it was still on my shoulder. As I was still struggling to take it back

23

from the thorns as I did not want to leave it there and run away because my jujus, gunpowder, etc., were inside it. The rest hunters ran to that direction and then he ("Odara") saw me held up there.

Immediately he saw me there he threw one of his poisonous cudgels to me but I snatched that one easily because it did not hit me, and he threw another one at the same time which hit my breast so heavily that I should had died at once if I had had no juju in my body. When he saw that the second one hit my breast he thought that no doubt I would die in a few minutes time and when he caught the rest hunters then he would come back to take me as well. But luckily immediately he left that place and as he was still chasing the rest hunters along. When I struggled very hard my hunting bag came out from the thorns, then without hesitation I took the two poisonous cudgels and I started to run away for my life as before.

After a few minutes, and as I was still running along zigzag in this jungle just to find out a safety place in which to hide myself before he would come back. I simply saw him as he was chasing the rest hunters towards the place that I was about to hide. Having seen this, I began to run to another part of the jungle at the same time. But those hunters were following me along at the same time instead to run to another place. So this cruel creature, "Odara" was then chasing the whole of us along at a time to catch and kill.

As he was chasing us along it was so he was throwing his cudgels to us repeatedly until we came to the road that which went along to those hunters' town. Then at the same moment we continued to run along on this road towards the town and he was still chasing us along as fast as he could until we came to a big river which was crossed this road. But as it was only one slender stick was put across the river with which the people of the town were crossing it so after we crossed it to the second side and when "Odara" walked on this slender stick to the middle of the river with greediness. The stick broke into two and then he fell into the water unexpectedly, because he was heavier than what the stick could hold. But as "Odara" was so greedy and cruel was that as he was struggling very hardly to come out from the water it was so he was still throwing his poisonous cudgels at us. Of course, after I shot my "shakabullah" gun to him several times and did not kill or harm him except the sound—"Shaka—bul—laha!" which was simply hearing. Then I started to throw some of his cudgels which he had thrown to us back to him until he sank into the water. It was like that I saw the end of this cruel creature, "Odara" the possessor of the poisonous cudgels.

I kept two of these poisonous cudgels with myself perhaps they would be useful to me in future. And after we rested for some minutes at the bank of this river those hunters told me to follow them to their town and I did so when I thought within myself that I would rest in that town for a few days when I would continue my journey direct to the Jungle of the Pigmies.

In the Ibembe Town

*The rain does not know the honourable person
apart. But the rain soaks anybody who comes out
when it is raining.*
    The bad bird that eats together with witches.

When I followed these hunters to their town, the
town which was called "Ibembe" and as it was the
custom of the people of this town that, any stranger
who came there must be taken to the king and tell the
king the kind of a person whom he or she was and to
tell the king as well what he or she came there for.
Therefore these hunters took me to their king dir-
ectly. But to my surprise was that as I was following
the hunters to the king, the whole people of this town
rushed out from their houses. They were following us
along and they were looking at me with great wonder when they saw that I put the gun and hunting bag
on my left shoulder like a hunter. They were asking
from one another that—"Is this a young lady huntress?" They asked this question with wonder because
they had never seen or ever heard of a lady who was a
huntress like me in their lives.

When I stood before the king and his chiefs and

within a few seconds that he (king) started to ask some questions from me thousands of people had gathered round and they were looking on with great wonder. The king asked from me that where was my town and I told him. He asked whether it was true that I was a huntress and I told him that it was true, I was a brave lady who was a huntress. But I wondered that I hardly explained like that when the whole people and the chiefs who were all the while looking at me with much astonishment, shouted on me at a time, that if it was true that I was a brave huntress it meant then I was a wicked lady who would be surely turned into a witch in future.

Again the king asked from me the name of the jungle in which I was going to hunt. But when I told him that I was going to hunt in the Jungle of the Pigmies, the whole people, the chiefs and the king himself covered their ears with their hands for a few minutes before they took their hands away from their ears and then they repeated with much surprise that—you a fine lady like this was going to hunt in the Jungle of the Pigmies and not in the ordinary jungle? and I replied—yes. Then the whole people did not laugh or talk but they were looking at me with sadness until when their king asked from me again whether I knew the kinds of the cruel and harmful creatures, apart from the wonderful wild animals, who were living in this jungle. I explained loudly to the king that before I left my town, the people of my town and my father had told me about the creatures of the jungle but I was not afraid of any creature who might be in the jungle. When I said like that the whole of them shrugged their shoulders in such a way which showed me that they were very sorry for me.

After that the king asked whether I would stay with him for a few days before I would continue my journey direct to the Jungle of the Pigmies and I told him that I would stay with him. Then he told one of his servants to put me in one of the rooms which were in the palace. The servant gave me the nice food and water at once and before I finished with the food it was about six o'clock in the evening.

When I finished with the food, I hung my hunting bag and cutlass on the stick which was nailed to the wall of this room and I leaned my "shakabullah" gun very carefully on one corner of this room as well. After that I went to the outside of the palace with the intention to take some breeze. But to my surprise and fear was that I saw that both the people and their children who had scattered to everywhere in the town, were running as hastily as they could back to their houses. They were closing the doors and windows immediately they were entering their houses. All the domestic animals were running here and there and they were hiding themselves as well. All the fires which were at outsides of the houses before that time were quenched with water at once before these people entered their houses. And within five minutes every part of the town was empty, there was no a single living creature could be seen again.

But as I was a stranger in this town who did not know what was going on there and as I did not return to the palace in time, so one of the servants stood at the gate of the palace and he called me quietly to enter the palace and I hardly entered when he hastily closed the gate. Then I entered my room, I sat down and I began to think within myself whether there was something happened in this town that evening or perhaps they did all this thing because I had told them that I was going to hunt in the Jungle of the Pigmies. But when I thought like that for a few minutes it came to my mind to ask what happened from this servant. It was not so long when I thought to do so when this servant was staggering about in the darkness. Then I called him. But when he entered the room he did not know the real part of the room that I sat. He was still finding me with hands when I asked from him that why there was no light at all in this palace. But instead to answer my question first he warned me very quietly that I must be talking gently.

When he traced me out he sat near me. Then I asked again that why the whole people of the town hid themselves in their houses as if something was coming to kill them and I asked as well that why there was no light neither in the palace nor in any part of the town. He explained to me that there was a terrible bird which was coming from the Jungle of the Pigmies to the town every night. He told me that whenever the bird came it would cry so loudly and terribly that the whole people of the town and the domestic animals would nearly die for fear, and if the bird saw any one or a domestic animal walking about in the town by that time, it would come down and take him or her away alive. This servant told me further that if the bird saw a house in which there was light or if it heard that the people of that house were talking, it would break the roof of that house with its beak and then take all the people of that house away alive. He told me furthermore that this bird was a mighty and curious one, because whenever it was coming to the town the noises and breeze of its wings would nearly to break down all the houses.

After this servant had explained to me like that I asked from him whether they had once tried to kill it with gun or with any weapon. But he told me that all the hunters of that town had tried to shoot it to death several times but they could not kill it because the gun could not kill it at all and instead to die it was carrying several hunters away each time that they attempted to kill it. He said that when it had nearly carried all the hunters of the town away then the rest feared and since then they never attempted to kill it.

When this servant explained to me as above I wondered greatly and then I told him at once that I would kill the bird if I saw it. When this servant heard so from me he was so surprised that he stood up at once and he staggered to the king who sat in the darkness as well. He told the king that I promised that I could kill the bird with my "shakabullah" gun. And when the king heard like that from him, he told him to go and call me for him and I went to him at once. He asked from me whether I made a promise that I could kill the bird and I told him that I could kill it. But he warned me very seriously that it was very dangerous if I failed to kill it, because it would take me away instead, but I made the promise before him again that I would not fail to kill it.

Then when it was the following evening, before this bad bird came, I made a big fire on the big field which was at the front of the palace. The flame of this fire shone to the great height in the sky and was easily seen from a long distance. After that I asked for a big pot which could contain me and they gave it to me. I cut a part of it like a round window and then I put it a little distance from the fire. After I loaded my gun I took one of the poisonous cudgels, which I took from "Odara" and then I covered myself with that pot and I was keeping watch of the bad bird through the round window.

Truly speaking, as the king had told me, when this bird was still in a distance of two miles I nearly died for fear and I nearly to give up my promise because the noises which its wings were making showed that indeed it was a bad and terrible bird which was bold enough that it was eating together with witches. When the noises were more hearing I believed that it was nearer and then I held my gun and the poisonous cudgel ready. Within a few minutes it came to the town and then it was flying about in the town perhaps it would see a person or a domestic animal to be taken away. But when it flew to the centre of the town, it saw this fire. And as it was a great surprise to it to see fire in this town by that time because such a thing had not happened before. Therefore it flew to the great height in the sky and then it cried very horribly just to make sure whether the person who made the fire was near there and to take him away. But it was a great wonder to it to hear that I answered or repeated its cry because there was none of the people of this town who was brave enough to make even a slight noise whenever it came.

To make sure again whether it was a human being who repeated its cry, then with great anger it said with another terrible voice—"I am a wonderful bad creature who is half human and half bird. I am so bad, bold, cruel and so brave that I am eating together with witches! I am one of the fears of the Jungle of the Pigmies! I am a bad semi-bird who has long sharp thorns on both my wings! My beak was so long and sharp that I have pierced several people to death with it! I am quite sure that there is no another living creature or human being in this world who is brave and cruel enough to challenge me in the night! I have already swallowed thousands of hunters who had attempted to kill me and it was so I had swallowed all the hunters who had come to hunt in the Jungle of the Pigmies!"

But before this semi-bird shouted terribly like that to the end, I nearly died for fear. Of course, when I remembered that—

Beard is the sign of old but moustache is the sign of insult.

So it had insulted its creator that night and by that if I tried to kill it, it would be easily for me to do so, because its boasts were insults to me. Therefore without hesitation I replied as thus—"Here is some one already who is waiting to challenge you and fight with you this night! I am ready to shoot you down now, although I am a huntress and not a hunter!

"I am a cruel huntress who has two poisonous cudgels and one fearful 'shakabullah' gun! Although you have long sharp beak and long sharp thorns on your wings with which you have killed thousands of hunters! But I shall see the end of you this night at all costs! Come down! Come down! Come down!" it was like that I replied this semi-bird very loudly without fear.

But he was greatly surprised to hear this hot challenge from me, because it had never heard any challenge from the people of this town since when it had started to come there and carry them away alive. But as it was coming down to the fire with full speed with intention to carry me away. I hastily shot my gun to him but he hastily flew back into the sky when the gun-shots cut some of his thorny wings away instead to hit his body. Again as he was coming down for the second time with great anger I shot him. But when the gun-shots hit his body this time, his body simply flung all the gun-shots away instead to kill him or to wound

33

him. It was like that I was shooting him repeatedly until when the gun-powder and gun-shots finished. To my surprise and fear was that my gun did nothing to him but it only prevented him from coming down and carry me away as he wished to do.

It was as from this night that I believed that when there were no gun-powder and gun-shots the gun became a mere stick, because as the gun on which I put all my hope had become useless or a mere stick then all my body began to tremble for fear of not being carried away by this cruel semi-bird. But God was so good, as I was just thinking in mind to come out from the pot with which I covered myself or protected myself all the while and then to run away perhaps I would be saved, luckily it came to my mind this moment to throw one of the two poisonous cudgels to him perhaps the poison which was in this cudgel would kill him.

Immediately I held the cudgel and I was expecting him to come down as he was doing before. A few minutes after that he did not hear the sound of my "shakabullah" gun again, he flew down. As he was looking round and round all over the spot just to find me out and then to carry me away, I hastily threw one of the poisonous cudgels to him. To my surprise and fear in the first instance was that when this cudgel hit him the poison which was in it only made him powerless to fly back to the sky but it did not kill him at all. And as this was a great danger to me so I hastily held the second cudgel, I came out from the pot and then I started to beat him with it. But as he was a mighty and powerful semi-bird he was also striking me with his long sharp beak repeatedly and he was scratching all my body with his thorny wings as well. We fought together for about two hours before he became entirely powerless and a few minutes after he died. It was like that I killed this half human and half bird. Although he hurt every part of my body with his sharp beak and thorny wings. And it was as from this night I began to take great care of these two poisonous cudgels because that was the first time I ever used them since when I had seized them when "Odara" the jungle giant, threw them to me. So when I saw that both would help me so much in future then I kept them.

In the morning, I showed the dead body of this semi-bird to the king and he was so much happy when he saw his dead body that he called the whole people of the town to come and see the dead body of their enemy. When the people saw that I had killed him they held me with gladness for a few minutes and they were greatly astonished to see a huntress like me who could do what thousands of hunters had failed to do. And on that spot several people gave me many expensive gifts.

It is after the elephant is dead when everybody will go near it and cut its flesh.

Because as this semi-bird was already dead the king and the people did not fear to approach him as when he was alive. After he (king) pulled out some of the wings and put them round his crown, just to be re-membering for ever that a semi-bird had once been carrying them away alive, then each of the people took some of the feathers to his or her house and kept them for the future. After the whole people had seen the dead body of this semi-bird and went back to their houses, then I took the two poisonous cudgels and my "shakabullah" gun and I went back to the palace. So as from that day the king and his people were taking great care of me as if I was their daughter.

I Became the Private Barber for the King of Ibembe Town

Whisper! so delicate to speak aloud like a secret word.
Ah! the head of the king sprouts two horns!

One morning, as I was thinking how to get the gun-powder and gun-shots and after that to continue my journey to the Jungle of the Pigmies, as I had used the whole of my gun-powder and gun-shots when I was shooting the gun to the late semi-bird the other night, the king called me to his private room. He asked me whether I still put in mind to go and hunt in the Jungle of the Pigmies. I replied at the same moment that I did not change my mind at any time not to go there because my family at home and the rest people of my town were with the hope now that I was already in the jungle.

After I explained to the king like that then I told him that if I had not been used the whole of my gun-powder and gun-shots, I would continue to go to the jungle tomorrow morning. When he heard like that from me he gave me plenty of gun-powder and

37

gun-shots. But he told me that I should stay with him for some months before I would continue my journey. He said that during the period that I would stay with him I would be his barber and that I would be barbing the hairs of his head every fortnight and that each time that I barbed his head he would be paying me one pound. He explained further that the reason why he would be paying me a large sum of money like that was that there was a strange thing which was on his head and which he did not like any of his townspeople to see otherwise he would engage one of the barbers who were in his town. He said that as I was a stranger and as I had no any friend there, therefore I would have no one there to whom I would leak out the secret of his head.

He warned me very seriously for three times that I must not leak out the secret to anybody or if he heard the secret from somebody he would kill me for it. But as he gave me plenty of gun-powder and gun-shots so I agreed to be his private barber and I promised him that I would not tell the secret of his head to any-body. Immediately I promised him like that he took off the crown which was on his head. To my greatest surprise and fear there were two thick short horns on his head. Immediately I saw that he had two horns on head I ran with fear to a short distance and I did not know when I shouted—"Ah! the head of the king sprouts two horns!" But he hastily covered my mouth with hands so that the other people might not over-hear. And then he warned very seriously again not to let his people know about the horns otherwise they would exile him at once.

The same day, he gave me the knife with which to clear the hairs off and I started to clear it at once. But as I was clearing it, it was so he was warning me repeatedly not to let the knife touch the two horns or if the knife touched them he would feel pain even nearly to death. And before I cleared the whole of the hairs I nearly fainted for fear because I had never seen a human being with horns on head since when I was born. These horns feared me even more than the semi-bird which I had killed.

This king was paying me one pound each time that I cleared the hairs for him and I did not leak out the secret of his head which sprouted two thick short horns to anybody. But since the first day that I had seen these two horns on his head I was unable to eat as well as before I had never seen them or as when I never knew that he had horns on head. And I was unable to sleep in the day and night because I was always thinking about his curious head which sprouted two horns.

Within a few weeks I was so leaned that everyone was saying that I was ill. I used many kinds of medicines but there was no change at all. At last when I believed that I would die in a few days time, then I went to an old man whose house was far away from the palace of the king. I told him that I did not know the reason why I was leaning more and more every day. This old man asked whether I was sick or I was doing hard work or I did not eat sufficient food. But I told him that I did no hard work and I was not sick but I could not eat as well as before and I could not sleep in the day and night. Then he asked me whether there was a serious matter which I was thinking in mind always and I said yes. Then he told me to tell him the matter so that he might advise me about it. When he said so I raised up my head and I looked at the sky and thought over for some minutes whether to tell him about the head of the king which sprouted the two horns and then I bent my head down I looked at the ground and I thought over for some minutes whether to leak out the secret to him but when I remembered that—"Whisperly the king spoke to me about the two horns of his head and if I leaked out the secret to this old man, surely, the king would hear and then he would kill me." So for this reason I did not tell him what I was thinking in mind. But when he hesitated for a while to tell him and I did not, then he told me that if the matter was so secrecy that I could not leak it out to him, I should go to the bush, I should dig a hole and then I should kneel down and speak out the matter to that hole and after that I should close the hole back with earth.

When this old man advised me like that I thanked him greatly and I went direct to the bush at once. I dug a huge pit and I said loudly into it—"The head of the king of Ibembe town sprouted two thick short horns!" After I leaked out this secret into this pit and I covered it back with the earth then I came back to the town. But to my surprise was that since when I had done so I did not think so much about the horns and within five days I became as normal as before.

The thief who steals bugle. Where is he going to blow it? In this world of the white men or in the heaven?

But there were many wonderful things in the days gone by, was that after a few days that I had leaked out the secret of the two horns which sprouted from the head of the king, to the pit, two young curious trees sprouted from that pit. Both were sprouted in form of twins and they were so beautiful that the man who first saw them cut them at once. This man was a bugle-blower.

When he cut them then he thought within himself for a few minutes that what could he do with beautiful curious young trees as these. Then at the same moment it came to his mind to carve them into a bugle and he did so. But immediately he put this bugle in mouth and he hardly blew a very slightly air in it when it spoke out loudly—

> "The head of the king of Ibembe sprouts two horns!
> The head of the king of Ibembe sprouts two horns!
> The two horns are thick and short!"

This bugle spoke out like that with a very lovely

tone and when this man heard this he was so happy or admired it that he ran with the bugle to the town. He went to the most senior chief who was next to the king. And when he blew this wonderful bugle before this chief he was so admired what it said that he took it from this man. He kept it for the day that the king would celebrate this birthday when they would blow it for the king and it would be the most important bugle which would be used on this day. This chief thought that the king would admire what it was saying as well because he (chief) did not know that the king had two horns on head which he did not want anybody to see.

By and by, the day that the king would celebrate his birthday was reached. After the whole people of the town and the chiefs had gathered at the front of the palace and when the king sat in the circle of the crowd. Then the bugle-blower started to blow this wonderful bugle repeatedly. But when the king heard what this bugle was saying—"The head of the king of Ibembe sprouts two horns! The two horns are thick and short!" he shrank up with great sorrow at the same moment. He looked at me with wild eyes. For he thought that I was the one who told the bugler that he had horns on head. Immediately this bugler started to blow this bugle and I heard what it was saying I winked my eyes to him to stop to blow it but he did not stop to blow it and then I waved hand to him to stop it but still he did not stop it.

As the bugler was still blowing this bugle, one of the chiefs who was wiser than the rest stood up, he went to the king and he took off the crown which was on the head of the king suddenly, just to make sure whether what the bugle was saying was true. But the whole people were greatly wondered and feared when they saw that their king had horns on head. And on the same spot some of the people said that they would exile the king and some said that it was better to cut the horns away instead to exile him but those who were the supporters of the king insisted that the king would not be exiled and the horns on his head would not be cut off. As they were still arguing within themselves those who were not the supporters of the king started to beat those who were supporters of the king. Within a few minutes there was a big and fearful riot in the town and the supporters of the king were chasing me about to kill when the king explained to them that I was the one who leaked out the secret of the two horns because I was his private hairdresser who had seen his head.

This riot was so fierce that the whole people had to leave this town for another town. But as everybody was leaving and the supporters of the king was still chasing me about to kill. Then I went back to the palace through the crooked way, I took my "shakabullah" gun, hunting bag, cutlass and the two poisonous cudgels and then I ran out from the palace. But as I was leaving the town as hastily as I could the supporters of the king saw me again. As they were chasing me along to kill and when I believed that they would overtake me very soon then I started to shoot them with my gun. But when several of them were wounded then they went back from me. It was like that I left this town and continued my journey unexpectedly to the Jungle of the Pigmies.

Please, Lay Your Head on this Rock and Let me cut it off at Once!

The fortune teller will die, the doctor will go to heaven and death will kill the sorcerer.

Adebisi cannot fight but she has sister (gun) who is fierce enough to help her.

After I had left Ibembe town and travelled about five miles, I stopped and sat down under a tree which had a very cool shadow. Luckily it was not so long from when I was thinking what to eat when I saw a big bird and I shot it down with my "shakabullah" gun. When I picked it up I saw that it was a bush pigeon. Then at the same time I made a fire under that tree and I roasted it with the fire and I ate the whole of it at a time because I was very hungry before I travelled to that place and I enjoyed it very nicely as it was fatty.

After I ate this bird I looked round there, I saw a pond, I went to it and I drank from the water which was in it to my satisfaction before I came back. Then I loaded my gun with gun-powder and gun-shots. But as I felt to rest for a few minutes therefore I leaned my back on the buttress of that tree and I did not know the time when I felt asleep when the cool air rushed to me. I enjoyed the sleep for about two hours before I woke up. At the same time I put my gun and hunting bag on my shoulder, I held the poisonous cudgels and my cutlass with the left hand and then I continued to travel along on this road. A few minutes after I travelled to the end of this road.

But when I travelled to the end of this road and still I never reached the jungle at all, even I never smelt it at all and again I did not know on which part of the bush that I would travel to the jungle. So I stopped near a rock when I remembered that my father had explained to me that there was no any hunter who could see the real road on which to travel to the jungle without other means. Therefore, I took out one wonderful juju from my hunting bag. This juju was the very one which my father had been using whenever he was going to this Jungle of the Pigmies. Whenever he travelled to where there was no road or whenever the road was ended suddenly, if he stretched up this juju, any direction that the breeze or air blew it to, was the right direction he should take. This juju was just like the tail of a big cow, it was very bushy and it was a very sure "juju-compass" which had never deceived my father once throughout the time that he hunted.

And when I stretched this inherited "juju-compass" up the breeze blew it to my left and then I started to travel to that direction at once. I travelled till the nightfall. But when the darkness did not allow me to see again, then I stopped, I climbed a big tree and I slept on its branches till the daybreak. But when I came down in the morning, I did not travel so far when I was seeing the Jungle of the Pigmies far away from me.

When I travelled as quickly as I could it was not more than twelve o'clock p.m. when I was seeing it clearly. Then I stopped I redressed all my dressings, I took my gun away from the shoulder, I held it tightly and then I continued to go along. Not knowing that I could not enter this jungle as easily as I had been thinking in my mind but before I would be able to enter it I would fight with all my power even perhaps I would die while I was still struggling to enter it.

Having travelled for about thirty minutes I saw the gate-keeper who stood firmly on the wide road on which I was travelling along. Immediately he saw me his eyes became very wild and he asked me without hesitation—"Who are you? Where are you going?" But with trembling voice I replied—"I am a huntress and I am going to hunt in the Jungle of the Pigmies." When he heard like that from me he repeated the name of the jungle—"In the Jungle of the Pigmies?" When he asked like that I could not reply with mouth but I could only reply with my head. After that he said quietly—"All right, come and lay your head on this rock and let me cut it off. I do not need yourself or the rest part of your body but your head."

Willing or not I was first going to him as he commanded me. But after a few seconds his fear stopped me at a little distance from him, because I was unable to lift up my feet and be going to him again. When I stopped and looked at him very well he was indeed "the heavy rain which stopped the voice of bird". Because I could not open my mouth and speak out any word for about ten minutes but I was simply looking at him and his surroundings with the fear that which I could not describe here yet.

When I looked at him very well I saw that he wore the skin or leather of buffalo which did not reach his knees and he did not cover the rest part of his body with anything. His body was full of big buoys, each of the buoys was as big as a fist. His legs were very thick and the arms were thick at about two feet diametre and all his body was full of thick veins which were stretched out very tightly as if they were going to cut soon. His eyes were so fearful that I could not look at them very well, he had no hairs on head at all but his beard was so plenty that it covered his neck and chest. His face did not show that he was laughing at all but it showed that he was cruel and harmful to every hunter or huntress or anybody who went there. He was so fat that he could not look here and there as fast as he wanted it to be. He was so short that he did not reach my waist and this showed me that he was a pigmy. His heavy head was helping him indeed whenever he wanted to kill a powerful creature because once he hit that creature with it, it would die at once.

And again when I glanced at the surroundings on which he stood, I saw that there were uncountable of bones of hunters and wild animals, and several heavy cudgels were lying all over the ground and plenty of heavy stones which were throwing to his victims, were also lying all over that spot. He always held one heavy cudgel which had a very big round head. And as he was talking to me it was so he was looking at the big round head of this cudgel and after a few minutes he would glance at my own head, and this showed me that he was thinking in mind that he was going to beat my head with this cudgel.

When I noticed that whenever he looked at the head of his cudgel he would look at my head as well and again when I saw all the fearful things which were surrounded him, my bravery flew away from my body and then great fear replaced it at once. Then I began to tremble from feet to head with fear. But when I was about to throw away my gun, hunting bag, etc., and then to start to run away for my life, it came to my mind suddenly this moment that all my four brothers were still held up in the custody of the pigmies and that it was in respect of them I was going to hunt in the Jungle of the Pigmies perhaps I would see them and bring them back to the town. When it came to my mind like that, my bravery returned to my body at the same time. And then I thought over again that—"Although I have jumped this well and I have jumped that well makes cat to fall into a well one day." This meant as this gate-keeper had killed several hunters, etc., but I as a huntress who had no power like those hunters, would by a surprise, kill him because it is a useless dog always kills hare.

When all these thoughts came to my mind

suddenly then I started to shout greatly on him—
"Please, the gate-keeper, open the gate for me and I
want to pass into the jungle!" But when he asked—
"To pass to where?" I told him very loudly—"To pass
to the Jungle of the Pigmies!" But instead to open
this gate and let me pass in he simply bursted into a great laughter and he said—"I believe you don't
know where you are yet! To open this gate for you
or what do you say now? Look at all these bones
and skulls! They are the bones and skulls of all the
hunters who had wanted to go to the jungle when
I killed them! Come to me and let me cut off your
head at once, you hopeless huntress!"

But when this gate-keeper shouted on me greatly
like that I was so annoyed that I did not know when
I shot my "shakabullah" gun at his head because I
thought that as his head had no hair at all the gun-
shots would be easily entered his brain and so by that
he would fall down and die at once. But to my surprise and fear the gun-shots were unable to enter into
his brain at all and instead of that they fell down before him. He picked them up and threw them back to
me without hesitation. Again he told me to shoot at
his head as many times as I liked and then he bent the
sparkling forehead towards me and he was expecting
more shots.

Again, without hesitation I loaded my gun and I
shot at his forehead for the second time. But to my
surprise, my gun only sounded—"Shaka—bul—laha"
and the gun-shots did not do anything to his head at

all. At last when I believed that my gun could not do anything to him then I put the gun down and I held one of the poisonous cudgels while my hunting bag was still on my shoulder, and then I told him that I was ready to fight with him. As I was doing that he had gathered some heavy stones and many cudgels into one place. After that he was coming to me direct and to beat me to death with the heavy cudgel which he held all the while.

As he raised up this cudgel just to beat me to death with it, I hastily jumped to his right and then I beat him heavily on the head with my poisonous cudgel. After he struggled and he turned to his right and when he was about to beat me with his heavy cudgel, I ran to his back unexpectedly and I hastily beat him on the head so heavily that he felt so much pain that he hesitated for a few minutes as if he was going to fall down and die. When he did so I thought he was entirely powerless and then I was beating him with the cudgel so repeatedly that I did not know the time that he stretched his hands backward and then he gripped my waist.

When he pressed my waist with both hands very hardly I nearly cut into two. I could not breathe in and out again and both my eyes were so opened widely with pain that I could not see again, and both were nearly to tear. And again, with anger he lifted the whole of me very high and then with all his power he flung me to where there was a big rock. His intention was that my head would hit that rock and then I would die at once. But it was a great surprise to him when he saw that my body did not even touch the rock before I stood upright and I was telling him loudly— "Cat never touch the ground with its back whenever it falls!" When he was hearing what I was saying repeatedly he became more angry and he ran to me and held my right leg unexpectedly. But as he was trying to tear it away from my body, it hooked his long beard and then I began to dangle here and there as he was trying to take it away from his beard as quickly as possible, because his lower jaw was then paining him very badly. When the pain was too much for him and my leg did not come out from his beard in time. He left it there but he was then running along to where he had made a big fire just to put me inside this fire so that I might be burnt to death at once, and after that to take my leg away from his beard as quickly as possible.

But when I saw that he was going to put me in the fire, I hastily held the branch of a tree which was on the way to the place of the fire. I held the branch of this tree so tightly with all my power that he could not go front or back. When I pulled up my leg it pulled up his beard as well. And when the pain was too severe for him he did not know when he began to climb up this tree along to me. And as he was coming up it was so I too were climbing on and on to the topmost of this tree. When he came nearer to me then I started to beat his head and jaws until when he be came powerless to hold the branch of the tree with his hands. But when he began to dangle then I took my leg away from his beard and then he fell from the top of this tree to the ground and he lay down helplessly.

When I came down I beat him again for a few minutes so that he might not be able to stand up until when I would leave there for the jungle. Of course he died after a few minutes.

It was like that I won this powerful gate-keeper, of course it was not easy for me before I saw the end of him. Because he attempted very hardly to kill me as he had killed several hunters, etc., and he did not know that—"I have jumped this well and I have jumped that well, one day the cat would fall into the well." But this day I killed him in return. After that I hung my gun and hunting bag on my shoulder, I took my cutlass and the poisonous cudgels and then I left there for another place. But it was the following morning before I passed through this gate to the Jungle of the Pigmies because I was so tired that I was unable to continue my journey the same day to this jungle.

In the Jungle of the Pigmies

*Before we can see the animal like that of
elephant will be in a very far jungle.*

*Before we can see the animal like that of
buffalo will be in a very far field.*

*And before we can see the bird like that of
peacock will be in the heaven.*

*But before we can see a jungle like that of the
Jungle of the Pigmies will be in the right place
as this.*

It was the "Day of Confusion" Wednesday, that I
entered this Jungle of the Pigmies, at about eleven
o'clock in the morning. After I travelled in this jungle
for a few minutes—the great fears, wonders, and uncountable of undescriptive strange things, which I was
seeing here and there were stopped me by force.
When I was unable to travel further because of these
things then I thought within myself to climb a tree
to the top so that I might see these things to my satisfaction. And at the same time I climbed a tall tree
to the top. I sat on one of its branches and as it was
a leafy tree therefore these leaves were covered me
and I peeped out very seriously as when an offender

peeped out from the small window of his cell. Then I was looking at these handiworks of God with great wonder.

When it was about twelve o'clock in the afternoon, the sun came. The heat of the sun was so hot that it forced all the living creatures to remain quietly in the places that they were. All the wild animals were kept quiet as if they were harmless. The lions stopped roaring but kept quiet as if they were dumbs. The birds of the sky were perched on the branches of the mighty tall trees, except those of the minute birds as canaries, migratory birds, etc., etc., which were jumping from one branch to another. Although the doves were crying in five minutes interval as they were telling the other creatures the right time (clock). Doves were the clocks of hunters because they never forget to remind or tell the hunters the right time. But as the owls were not coming out in the daytime or if they did come out or fly in the daytime and if a hunter saw it, it was a bad sign indeed. It was so their hoot was a great help to the hunters. Because their hoot was driving animals to the hunters and it (hoot) was also amusing the hunters as they (hunters) had no partners in the jungle.

And all these creatures were kept quiet where they were for the sun was too hot. Because the sun of this jungle was also very curious. Whenever it was out it would be as hot as fire and that was why these living creatures were hiding themselves from it whenever it was out.

When I sat on the branch of this tree and I did not

see any living creature to move or walk about by that time and as the jungle was as calm as if there were none living creatures, then I was enjoying the peaceful cool breeze which my creator was sending to me. After a while I was feeling to eat, I was hungry badly. But to my surprise, as I was just thinking in mind what I could eat, one big edible fruit fell on to my head from the topmost branch of this tree. I took it and I ate it at once.

But when I raised up my head I saw that there were still many of this fruit on another branch of this tree. So I climbed that branch again, I sat down on it and then I started to eat the fruits one by one until when I was satisfied. After that I continued to look at the wonderful things of this jungle. And again I saw that the thick smoke was very common to see rushing out from the ground which was near the big trees, hills, rivers, ponds, etc. As this thick smoke was rushing out in large quantity it was so the sweet smell of food was rushing out as well and this showed me that many of the pigmies who were the inhabitants and owners of this jungle were living under the ground.

Truly speaking—"Before we can see the animal like that of elephant will be in a very far jungle and before we can see a jungle like that of the Jungle of the Pigmies will be in the right place as this" because when it was three o'clock p.m. prompt, there I heard suddenly that a bugle was blown from a long distance as I was still looking at the wonders of the jungle. The tone of this bugle was so powerful that it was heard clearly everywhere in the jungle and it shook both ground and mighty trees. A few seconds after the bugle had blasted, there I saw that a very strong wind started to blow. In this wind there I saw that animals, big birds, pigmies, etc., of this jungle were running up and down and they were making fearful noises all over the jungle. As the wind was stronger it was so they were making more fearful noises and within five minutes the whole of the jungle was in disorder.

After a while all the trees were blowing here and there, they were touching the ground with their tops. As I still held the branch of the tree on which I was so tightly that I might not fall down, the wild animals as lions, tigers, wolves, etc., came to that spot. As they were running to and fro, they raised up their heads and they were sniffing my smell. After a while they saw me as I sat on the branch of that tree and by this time their attitudes were more terrible because they wanted to eat me. As they were surrounded the tree closely it was so the strong wind was forcing it to touch the ground repeatedly. Each time that it touched the ground these wild animals were hastily jumping to where I sat on the branch, but they were unable to touch me before the tree would stand up-right again. It was like that these wild animals were jumping to me every time that the tree was bending down and getting up again. Luckily they were unable to take me away from the top of this tree until when the strong wind was stopped at about seven o'clock in the evening. But as their attitudes were too terrible so I shouted with fear until my voice was not heard clearly again before the wind was stopped. I attempted to be shooting these wild animals to death with my gun but the wind was blowing the tree so swiftly that I was unable to sight anything by that time.

But after the wind stopped blowing and all the trees stood quietly, I thought that these wild animals would go away but they did not attempt, they surrounded the tree and were looking at me as I sat on the branch of that tree. When I believed that they would not attempt to go away, then I began to shoot them with my "shakabullah" gun and when I killed nearly half of them the rest went away with fear. When I kept watch for a few minutes perhaps they hid near there but they had gone away then I came down from this tree. I took the smallest one of those which I killed and then I left that area as soon as possible.

When I travelled far away in the darkness, as it was then nine o'clock, for I heard when a dove gave the sign of time by that time. So I stopped under a tree which was almost covered by the running plants. I made a big fire, after I cut that animal into several parts then I started to roast them with this fire. One hour later they were roasted enough and I ate as much as I could from them. After that I gathered refuses and dried leaves together near this fire, I lay down on them, I put my head on my hunting bag as if it was a pillow. I lay the two poisonous cudgels at my left and my gun at my right, but I still held it with fear until I fell asleep unnoticed.

Of course, I was woken very early in the morning with great fear of the numerous birds which were surrounded me and they were crying repeatedly because I was curious to them. At the same time that I woke and I saw that I was already surrounded by these birds, I simply took my gun, hunting bag, cudgels and my cutlass and I left that spot. But to my fear these birds were still following me and they were still crying with their loudest voices. I was running away from them so that they might not suspect me to those super-human creatures. Luckily when I travelled to the darkest part of this jungle they could not see me again and then they went back from me.

It was like that I was travelling along and I was looking here and there perhaps I would see my four brothers in respect of whom I came to hunt in this jungle, till the light of the sun came down to all over the jungle when it was about nine o'clock and then I stopped. But when I felt to eat and there was nothing inside my hunting bag to eat. I started to look for a small animal to be killed. After a while I came across a small porcupine and I shot it to death at once. I made a fire and I roasted it in it and I ate the whole of it at a time because it was fatty. After I ate the porcupine to my satisfaction, I began to think in mind whether to kill the whole of the wild animals first, which would be the great obstacles to me when I would be looking for my four brothers or to be looking for my brothers first, before I would come back to these wild animals or to be looking for where the pigmies were living in this jungle first before I would come back to kill those wild animals. Because I ought to do all these three works—"To see that I kill the whole of the wild animals. To see that I kill the whole of the pigmies who were detaining many hunters or to drive them away from this jungle and the third work was to see that I bring my four brothers back to my town, because I had promised my people and the people of my town to do these three works before I left them for this jungle."

After a while it came to my mind to see that I killed the whole of the wild animals first so that there would be no any obstacle for me when I would start to look for my brothers and the pigmies. But immediately I concluded this thought, to my fear there I saw that a very small round hill which was at a little distance from me, splitted or parted into two suddenly and at the same moment a heavy black smoke was rushing out in large quantity. When I saw this again I feared greatly and I started to take all my things and then to leave there at once. But I was unable to take the whole of them when I saw that this smoke had covered the whole of that area and I could not see well as before. And as I was running along just to go out of this smoke, because I believed that no doubt something which was dangerous would come out of it very soon. As I was mistakingly dashing to both trees and rocks and all these things were distopping me to go out of this fearful smoke in time, I did not know when several creeping plants were twisted to both my legs in such a way that I fell down heavily unexpectedly. My gun, cudgels and cutlass were sprung away from me. But as I was hastily trying to take myself away from these ropes and then to continue to be running away for my life as before, there I saw a huge man appearing from this thick smoke and he was coming to me direct and I was greatly feared immediately I saw him.

This huge man was one of the "obstacles" of this jungle. He was one of the strongest and the most cruel pigmies who were keeping watch of the jungle always. His work was to be bringing any hunter or anyone who came to the jungle, to the town of the pigmies, for punishment. And indeed this huge pigmy was the "obstacle" of this jungle because he was too cruel and fearful. He was so huge and short that if he stood at a distance you could not believe that he was a living creature but the stump of a mighty tree. Each of his fingers was as big as a big plantain and it was permanently slightly curved. His arms were very long and thick. He had a big half fall goitre on his neck and he had a very big belly which, whenever he was going or running along, would be shaking here and there and sounding heavily.

Before he reached the place that I was held up by the ropes or the creeping plants, I had taken these creeping plants away from my legs and I had taken my gun, cudgels and my cutlass and then I continued to run away as before. As he was chasing me along to catch and when his palms were touching me slightly, then I started to run to left. But to my surprise there

I saw him at my front, he was laughing and coming to me. When I saw him that he did so I ran to my right perhaps I would be saved. But to my fear again I saw "obstacle" with heavy cudgel in hand and he appeared at my front and before I could do anything which could prevent me from him again he had held me and given me several slaps on both ears. Having done that for a few minutes then he mercilessly flung me away. And I dashed to a big tree which was near by and my head hit this tree so heavily that I was unable to stand up for some minutes.

When I believed that he had already caught me and I could not run away from him any more so I prepared to wait and fight with him to the last point. Although I could not conquer him but when I remembered that—"Adebisi is lazy to fight but she has a bold sister who is helping her to fight her enemies" and that was my "shakabullah" gun, then I became brave again. Therefore, at the same time I leaned my gun and the poisonous cudgels on the tree under which I was going to fight him. After that I told him loudly and without fear that he should come along and I was ready to fight with him and he came to me with the intention that he would easily kill me within a few seconds.

We first wrestled for about fifteen minutes. And each time that he was flinging me away with great anger, to his surprise, I was standing up and gripping him before my feet were touching the ground. He raised me very high and he flung me to a rock, with the intention that I would die at the same time, but I hastily held his big goitre when I was about to hit that rock, but both of us were slightly hit the rock instead, of course none of us had any injury. Within a few minutes we had scattered away all the dried leaves and refuses of that spot with our feet. After a while I became tired but "obstacle" did not. When I had no more power I loosened both my hands away from his body by force and then I ran to where I leaned the gun and I shot him unexpectedly. But to my surprise and fear was that my "shakabullah" gun simply sounded—"shaka—bul—laha" but I saw no where the gun-shots hit him.

When he saw that I shot him, he stood on one place, he was looking and laughing at me and this showed me that he was thinking in mind that I believed my gun was a harmful thing which could harm him, because he looked at the gun as if it was a mere stick. Again, as he was still looking on, I ran to the tree on which I leaned the two poisonous cudgels, I took one and with all my power I beat "obstacle" with it, for I thought the poison of this cudgel would kill him. But to my surprise this cudgel simply broke into several pieces instead to kill or make him powerless, and he was still greatly laughing at me.

When I believed that my gun and the poisonous cudgel could not do anything to "obstacle" then I sat down on the prop of the tree under which we were fighting. I was thinking how to safe myself from him. Although I still had many kinds of the charms or incantations in my mind but my mind was not at rest this moment to remember any of them. As I was still resting and thinking what to do again, he ran to me and he cut away my left foot unexpectedly. When he cut it off I fell down at once and I was crying loudly for pain. As I was doing like that and blaming myself that if I had known I should had not come to the Jungle of the Pigmies, he came and stood at my front. After he listened to what I said he bursted into a great laugh which lasted for about thirty minutes. At last when I could no longer bear the pain I shouted greatly for help because I believed that within a few minutes I might die.

To my surprise I hardly shouted for help when I saw that many pigmies like this "obstacle" gathered round me. But instead to help me fight him, all of them were laughing at me and were telling him repeatedly to cut my head away as well, but luckily he told them that he would not do so because he wanted to take me to their town. Having explained like that he simply picked up my left foot which he had cut away, he touched it with the remaining stump and to my surprise both were joined together at once as if it was not cut away before and I felt no pain again.

After he did so he wanted to take me to their town, for he thought I had already entirely powerless. But when I believed that once he took me to their town, there I would remain throughout my life time. Then I held the tree under which we were fighting with all my power. He was pulling me with all his power but I did not loose my hands away from this tree. As he was trying hardly to take me away it was so I was shouting greatly that you would not take me away and he too was saying that at all costs he would take me away. And as both of us were pulling each other to and fro in a very rough way, and it was like that we were doing until when he overpowered me. But God was so good as he was dragging me along as hastily as he could he did not know when he hit his head on the branch of a tree which was full of bees and wasps. When they covered him and were stinging him bitterly, he did not know when he left my hands and then he started to defend himself from these insects. But as he was defending himself it was so these insects were increasing and stinging him badly. As he was still staggering here and there I hastily ran back to the tree on which I leaned my gun. I loaded it with plenty of gun-powder and gun-shots, I ran back to him and I shot him on the head. So he fell down and died after a few minutes. That was how I conquered "obstacle". After that I left that area at once.

The Animal that Died but his Eyes still Alive

The big gun that stops the voices of the soldiers.
Animals are surplus in the town in which the
people have no teeth.

After I killed "obstacle" I travelled in this jungle till six
o'clock in the evening. As I was travelling along it was
so I was killing all the wild animals that I was seeing
on the way. When I saw that the night was approaching I shot one small animal to death. I made a big fire
and I roasted this animal which was an antelope, in
the fire. Before I ate it to my satisfaction it was about
ten o'clock in the night. But anyhow I ate out of it as
I could and I kept the rest of it near the fire which I
would eat in the morning. After that I lay down near
this fire and then I slept but there was nothing which
was happened to me throughout this night.

When I woke up in the morning by the crying
of birds and when the dove gave the sign of eight
o'clock, then I ate the rest of that roasted animal.
After that I hung my gun and hunting bag on my
shoulder having checked the gun and saw that it was
in good order. Then I started to look for the wild
animals to be killed. And within three days I nearly

killed the whole of the wild animals of this jungle. It was very scarcely to see one or two and I was very happy about this, but it still remained three big troubles—how to drive away all the pigmies from this jungle as they used to detain hunters in their custody. How to kill the dangerous animals who had light on eyes and how to kill a very curious and dangerous boa constrictor which was very dangerous to the hunters as well.

After I nearly killed the whole of the wild animals, I did not travel more than seven days when I came across a big wild animal. It was as big as an elephant. I had never seen the kind of this animal before. Because he had a very big head. Several horns were on his forehead. Each of the horns was as long and thick and sharp as cows' horns. Very long black and brown hairs were full this head and they were fallen downward, they were also very dirty. All the horns were stood upright on his forehead as if a person carried a bunch of sticks vertically. His beard was so plenty and long that it covered his chest and belly as well. The teeth of his mouth were so plenty and long that whenever he was eating a person who was in two miles away would be hearing the noises which they were making. Even as the teeth and the horns of his mouth and head were so fearful many of the wild animals who saw him when he was coming to kill them with all these things were dying for themselves before he would reach them instead to kill them with his teeth and horns, because they were too fearful to them.

He had two curious eyes which were as accurate as full moon of the dry season. Both were on the right part of his head as the other animals did, but each was bigger and could see everywhere without moving head. The powerful light that these eyes were bringing out could not go far or straight but they were bringing out the clear and round light. The ray of this light was always round him and it could be seen clearly from a long distance.

He had a kind of a terrible shout with which he was frightening the animals and his humming was also terrible to hear. All the rest animals were so hated and feared him that they never went near the place that he travelled for one week.

There was none part of his body which was not terrible and which was not frightened neither human being nor other creature of this world.

Immediately I saw this "super-animal" as I could call him, in that morning through the round clear light of his eyes, was that I stopped in one place and I first breathed out heavily with great fear. Because I could not escape again, I had already approached him too closely before I saw him. And at the same moment that he too saw me, although I was still quite aloof when he first saw me. He first sighted all his horns towards me and then he was running to me as fast as he could. But when I thought within myself that if I stood on the ground and shot him, he would kill me instantaneously, because my "shakabul-lah" gun would not be able to kill him in one shot, therefore I hastily climbed a tree to the top.

But when he ran to the place that I had stood before and he did not meet me there again. He was going round and round until when he saw me on top of this tree. As I was on top of this tree I thought that I was saved but not at all. Because at the same moment that he saw me on top of this tree, he started to bite the tree at the bottom. And to my fear within two minutes he had nearly bitten the whole bottom of this tree. When I saw that the tree was just toppling to the ground, just to safe my life, I hastily jumped from there to the top of another mighty tree which was nearby. And when he saw me on top of this mighty tree again, he started to bite the bottom of it as well and he was in great anger this time because he wanted to eat me without much trouble as this.

And when I saw that this mighty tree was toppling down as well, then I hastily sold my "death", I said within myself that before this "super-animal" would kill me I must first defend myself perhaps I would be saved. Then without hesitation I shot him. But when the gun-shots hit him on the chest and hurt him as well on the hind legs. It was this time this "super-animal" became more powerful and more dangerous than ever. And it was this day that I believed that—the half killed snake is the most dangerous. Because this animal was then shrieking and shouting and humming more terribly with angry voice than ever. His fearful humming was hearing all over the jungle.

He was jumping and dashing to the trees, rocks,

etc. and within a few minutes he had broken down all the trees of that area and scattered everything in disorder with great anger. When he came back to the tree on top of which I was he started to bite the bottom of this tree until it fell down. This tree hardly fell down when he jumped on me, but I was so lucky that immediately this tree fell on hard ground, it sprang up again before it lay down quietly, I fell off from it to a little distance, so by that he missed me to grip with his paws. Of course I hit my back on another tree which was near that spot and that gave me much pain. And as I was hastily standing up he had jumped high up and as he was coming down just to cover the whole of me, I hastily lay flatly on the ground and then he simply rolled along on the ground instead. Before he stood up again I had taken my cutlass and I was waiting for him at once.

Within one second he had stood up, but he did not attempt to bite me this time, he wanted to hit me to death with his horns. But at the same moment that I saw what he wanted to do this time, I hastily leapt to my left when he was about to butt me with his horns and I cut him several times with my cutlass within this moment, so he simply butted a heavy rock instead when he missed me. He hardly missed me when he turned to his back and as he was coming again with great anger, I hastily leaned my back on the stump of the big tree which he had cut down, and I exposed my chest and belly in such a deceived way that he believed that he would not miss me as before. So as he was running furiously towards me with all his power and when he was about to reach me, I hastily leapt again to my right unexpectedly and unfortunately he simply butted the stump of that tree. So all his horns pierced this stump of tree, he could not pull them out but he was held up there helplessly, except his hind legs with which he was scattering the ground very roughly.

After I rested for a few minutes then I started to beat him with my poisonous cudgel until when he was completely powerless and then he died after some minutes. It was like that I killed this "super-animal" as I could call him. But to my surprise was that as he had already dead the light of his eyes was still shining clearly and thus it was when I left there.

After I had killed this animal I started to look about for the fearful boa constrictor which my father had told me about his news that he (boa) was also very dangerous. As I was looking for this boa constrictor it was so I was killing all the wild animals which I was seeing on the way. And in a few days time I killed the whole of them. So this time there was no more the fear of the wild animals again in this jungle except the fears of this terrible boa constrictor and the pigmies. I roamed about for several days but I did not come across this boa until one day when I travelled back to the place where I had killed "super-animal" unnoticed. But it was still a great surprise to see that the light of the eyes of this animal was still shining clearly. The flesh of his body was already decayed and the bones were already scattered on the ground but the eyes which brought out this light was still alive, the light was as clear as when the animal was still alive. So the eyes and the long hairs which were covered the skull were still on this skull as well and all the horns were still on the skull but they were still pierced the stump of that tree since the day that the animal had butted it (stump) himself.

In the first instance that I came there unexpectedly and when I saw this head with the clear light I thought that the animal had become alive after I had left there the other day. I stood before this head and I started to think of what to do with it, because the clear light which came out from the eyes was very attractively. When I thought what to do with it for a few minutes and I did not know yet so I pulled the head out of the stump. I first trimmed the hairs of the head very short then I cut those long horns very short too after that I trimmed the inside of the skull very neatly. But to my surprise when I put this skull or head on my head it was my exact size and it seemed on my head as a cock helmet. I was seeing clearly through the eyes and the light of the eyes travelled far away in the jungle but I was then so fearful that there was no any living creature which would see me would not run away for fear because I was exactly as when that animal was alive. So when I believed that it would help me in future I wrapped it with the skin of animal and I kept it in my hunting bag. As from that day I was using it in the night as my light and I was wearing it on the head whenever I was hunting. So this wonderful head became a very useful thing at last.

72

The Huge Stern Pigmy
Captured Me

We must first greet the mother of a new born baby whether her baby will die soon or not.

If wild boar acts as rudely as pig does, he (wild boar) will ruin the town. And if slave becomes king the people will not remain—He will revenge.

After I wrapped this wonderful head and put it inside my hunting bag I travelled towards the north of the jungle, because this day was "The Day of New Creation" which was Thursday. As I was travelling along it was so I was looking for the fearful boa constrictor to be killed but I did not see it until I travelled about eight miles. When I travelled further I came to where there were plenty of the vast hills, mountains, and very rough mighty rocks which were as high and vast as mountains. There were several paths which went along to the inside of each of these vast rocks and this showed me that there were towns inside the bottoms of the rocks.

All the paths which went to the inside of each of these rocks were very clean, but many fearful things like images of giants, wild animals, big snakes, etc., were put on both sides of each of the paths. Complete skeletons of apes, tigers, human beings, etc., were also put on both sides of the paths. All these things were just warnings for another kinds of creatures not to enter or go near the rocks. But as I was unable to travel farther when I travelled to these rocks, etc., because I had already tired and again the night was approaching. So for this reason I stopped near the corner of one of these rocks. This corner was just as a room with a flat stone as its roof. Then I leaned my gun and the poisonous cudgel on the rock which was a wall for this room and I hung my hunting bag on it as well.

After that I gathered dried sticks together, I made fire in them and I roasted the edible fruits which I picked on the way along to these rocks. Having eaten the fruits to my satisfaction then I slept. Of course I saw several small animals on my way coming to these rocks but I did not attempt to kill any one of them for my food because I had tired of eating animals every day, for I did not see another thing to eat since when I had entered this jungle. Throughout that night there was nothing happened to me but I was dreaming of those images, etc., which were put on both sides of the paths. In my dreams, all these terrible images, etc., were chasing me about to kill. It was so they were troubling me until one of them which was the skelet-ons of a giant caught me and as he wanted to stab me at belly, so I woke with great fear but when I stood up and opened my eyes with fear I saw that it was already the daybreak and it was that time it just revealed to me that I had been just dreaming and all what I was seeing were not truth.

When I woke up I went to the spot where there were plenty of wild grasses. As I believed that these kind of grasses were always holding the dew which was falling down from the sky in the night. And as there was no pond or river from which I could get water, so I collected the dew which was on these grasses into a big snail shell until when the shell was full. After that I came back to the fire. Out of the dew I washed my face and I drank the rest after I ate another fruits which I roasted.

But I hardly finished with these roasted fruits when I began to hear the mixed noises of people from the bottom of this rock. The noises were just like that of a big town. But anyhow, as "We must first greet the mother of a new born baby whether her baby was going to die soon or would not die" therefore I waited there until I finished my fruits. After I ate the fruits and I was still hearing the noises I thought within myself that perhaps if I kept longer than that in this spot some of the creatures who were living under this rock might come out and when they met me there they might kill me. So I took all my things and I left there at once.

As I was going along it was so I was stumbling my right foot thumb on the ground after a few minutes interval and this was a very bad omen. Again several birds were flying past my head and everyone of them was striking my eyes with its wings and this was a very bad sign indeed. I became so sad when I saw all these bad signs that my body became very weak at the same time, because I believed that no doubt I would be in a trouble very soon. Especially as I was a huntress these kinds of signs were dangerous to happen to me and again when I remembered that this day was "The Day of Trouble" which was Friday, my body became more weak and I was then quite sure that the trouble which I was going to meet soon would be very serious.

Anyhow after I thought over that a person never died twice and that if I died I would go to heaven, then I sold my "death" and I continued to travel along as hastily as before I saw all these signs. When I travelled till nine o'clock a.m. then I began to look for small animals to be killed for my food. But I wondered greatly that I did not come across them except those squirrels which were barking at me here and there. I did not know whether as these squirrels were barking at me repeatedly their noises were suspecting me to these small animals and by that they were hiding themselves before I was travelling to where they were. But when it came to my mind like that I stopped when I travelled to a big tree which had many big buttresses. Then I cut plenty of broad leaves. When I knelt down behind one of the buttresses of this tree, I held these broad leaves with teeth in such a way that they covered my face and the rest part of my body, so that these animals might not see me again, but they might think that I was a plant.

Having done so I began to keep watch of the animals. Of course as I was doing this thing it was so I was thinking in mind of all the signs which I had seen on the way before I travelled to this tree. Because I believed that no doubt a very bad thing must happen to me before the night of this day.

It was like that I knelt down and I was keeping watch of the small animals for good two hours without seeing anything like animals except those squirrels which were hung near me and barking at me repeatedly. But when I was tired to wait for these animals and as I was just thinking in mind to stand up and go away from there. Then these animals began to pass through that place in great number, but they were running here and there as if somebody was driving them to somewhere, none of them hesitated in one place so that I might shoot it. But after a few minutes some of them were hesitating in one place for a few seconds and at the same moment that I sighted one of them to shoot. There appeared a stern huge pigmy from an unknown place. He was shouting greatly and continuously and his shout was driving these animals to another part of the jungle.

It was a great anger to me when it was the very moment that I wanted to shoot those animals that this stern pigmy began to shout greatly. For this reason I said with anger that "We must first greet the mother of a new born baby for safety delivery whether her baby would still die soon or not", which meant if this pigmy would kill me or not I must challenge him first.

And at the same moment that he travelled with shout to where I hid myself I asked from him with great anger—"By the way, you this stern huge pigmy, what are you shouting for? You hopeless thing!" When he heard like that he first bent down and peeped to where I hid just to make sure whom I was. Because the leaves with which I covered myself did not allow him to see me but he was just hearing my voice. When he saw me there, he kept quiet and looked at me thoroughly with wonder for about five minutes for in the first instance he could not say whether I was a pigmy like himself.

To make sure the kind of a creature that I was he asked from me with his native language—"Who are you? Will you come out and let me see you?" But when I could not answer him and I did not come out as he told me. He came to me with anger. And when he saw that I was a huntress, with gun, etc., in hand, he gripped my neck as if a giant gripped a grain of maize. He dragged me out of the place that I hid with anger and he still held my neck when he said loudly—"Oh, you too, come to steal our animals away! All right, I will take you too to where the rest of you are in the punishment since past ten years!"

As he held and pressed my neck so hardly that I could not even breathe in or out easily, he took my gun, hunting bag, the wonderful head of the animal which I wrapped with the skin of animal, the cudgel and cutlass from me. After that he tossed me without mercy to a short distance from this spot and my head was so struck the bottom of a tree that I could not stand up or even to raise up my head a little bit when he cut a strong rope. Then he came to me, he pulled me upright, he put both my hands to my back and then he tied both together with this rope. Having done that he hung my hunting bag and the head of the animal on his shoulder, but he did not loose the bag and the head of the animal which I wrapped, to know what were in them and he did not attempt to shoot or touch the trigger of my gun before he put it on his shoulder as well, of course I could not say whether he knew how to shoot gun or whether he had seen a gun before. After this he cut a long and strong whip with my cutlass. Having done this he held the cutlass and the cudgel with left hand and he held the whip with right hand.

After he stretched this whip to the direction that which he wanted me to be travelling along. When I was travelling along on that direction he followed me and he began to whip me mercilessly along to this direction. This direction went along to the vast rocks and mountains from where I had come to the very spot that he caught me. As I was going along with my hands which were tied very tightly toward my back it was so this huge pigmy was whipping me mercilessly. Whenever I missed the right direction on which he wanted me to travel, he would give me several heavy slaps on the ears. I was falling into the pits which were on this direction as he was pushing me along with his big navel, because he had no spare hand again with which to help himself, he held my things with them.

79

His navel was big that it could contain more than four gallons of water. It swelled out from his belly to a distance of about five feet. In respect of this fearful navel he was not wearing other cloth on his body except a big apron. Whenever he was walking very hastily along, this navel would be shaking and sounding heavily as when the water was shaking in a large tube and it appeared on his belly as if a very large bowl covered the belly.

As he was following me along and flogging me repeatedly, it was so he was shouting horribly on me—"Thief! thief! thief! I catch you today! All days are for thief to thieve but one day is for the owner to catch the thief!" It was like that this stern huge pigmy was shouting on me greatly.

When this punishment was too severe for me then I became powerless to walk after a short time. I was unable to go along any longer. When he saw this, he started to push me along with his fearful large navel and I was staggering along powerlessly. After a while I began to beg him for mercy but to my surprise was that the more I begged him the more the punishment he would give me would be severe. Not knowing that he hated to hear like that, it was a great anger to him. But at last when I begged him and he did not stop to flog me I told him that "If wild boar acts as rudely as pig does he (wild boar) will ruin the town" and if the rest pigmies like yourself had acted as rudely as you are illtreating me now, they (the rest pigmies) should had killed you. And I told him as well that if he had become a king all the people of his town would not remain in a few months time for his illtreatment.

When he heard all these words from me the punishment which he was then giving me was more severe than before. It was like that he was pushing me along with his navel as hastily as he could until when he pushed me to these vast rocks and mountains and without hesitation he pushed me like this into one of the vast rocks. It was this time I knew that he was one of the inhabitants of this rock, under which there was a big town of pigmies. And immediately he was pushing me along on the road which went along to this town, I said within myself that no doubt the pigmies would punish me to death in a few days time.

Uncountable of wild animals as lions, tigers, buffaloes, wolves, etc., and uncountable of the poisonous reptiles as boa constrictors, pythons, alligators, etc., were full up on this road. As he was still pushing me along they were rushing to me just to kill or swallow me but when they saw that it was this pigmy who was pushing me along, they would not do anything to me but they were parting to both sides of the road for us to pass. I believed that all these creatures were also the keepers of this road. They were killing and eating all the enemies of these pigmies.

As the attitudes of these creatures were too horrible for me as we were meeting them on this road, so whenever I feared and ran to either sides of the road, this pigmy would whip me very severely at the same time and then he would shout greatly that—"just be going along, you don't see wonders yet, you thief of animals!" After one and a halve hours we came to the gate of the town. The door of this gate was so strong and heavy that twenty men could not even push it to one side. But the gate-keeper was an ape. This ape was as strong as a giant. Of course he was not tall but he was so stout that he was easily opening and closing the door of this gate. When he pushed me with his fearful big navel to this gate and it was closed by that time, he knocked it with all his power. Then the ape or gate-keeper came out from the small house which was near the gate, he opened the door and then this pigmy pushed me in. But when this ape saw me he looked at me so savagely that I nearly fell down with fear. And when he rushed furiously against me and he raised up his heavy foot just to crush me to death at once, this stern huge pigmy hastily waved hand to him to leave me. Then he (ape) shut the door back, after that he entered that small house but he was still looking at me afar with his savage eyes.

So all these dangers of this road showed me that once an offender like myself was taken to this town, there was no doubt, if he or she attempted to run away would be killed on the road by these ape or the wild animals, etc., or it was entirely impossible for an offender to escape safely out of this town.

My Life in the Town of the Pigmies
—the Town Under the Rock

Animals surplus in the town where the people have no teeth.

One who is too old in tailoring work, will first look very sternly before he will be able to cut suits accurately or if he has money to buy spectacle, he will not look sternly before he will be able to cut suits accurately.

As this pigmy was pushing me along in the town, uncountable pigmies like himself were shouting on me—"Ah, this is another one of the thieves of animals!" They were making a mock and deriding of me, and it was so I was breathing quickly and audibly because I was so tired that I was unable to move my feet again for the severe punishment which this stern huge pigmy gave me was too much. And as he was pushing me along I noticed that the domestic animals of this town were outnumbered the pigmies and this showed me that they were not killing these animals for their food at all. And I first thought that perhaps these pigmies had no teeth with which to eat these animals and that was the reason these animals were surplus like that, because in the town where the people had teeth

83

the domestic animals never surplus as these.

After a while he pushed me to the palace of their king. Immediately he pushed me before the king he left me alone to stand, but I was powerless and I was unable to control myself so that I fell down at the same time and I was throbbing with great fear perhaps the king would give him the order to go and kill me. But luckily after the king heard the story of how he caught me from the jungle he ordered him to take me to their custody which was behind the town. Then this pigmy handed over my gun, hunting bag, the head of the animal which I wrapped with the skin of animal, the poisonous cudgel and my cutlass to the king and on my presence another pigmy climbed the ceiling of this palace and he put all my property there. The king did not attempt to know the contents of the bag, etc. as well as this stern huge pigmy. I noticed as well that in this ceiling there were many "shaka-bullah" guns, hunting bags, cutlasses, etc., which were taken from the hunters who had come to this jungle before I too came there. Of course I did not know whether my four brothers' guns, etc., in respect of whom I came to hunt in this jungle, were among these guns, etc.

Before I was taken out of the palace I noticed as well that this king was so old that his eyes could not see well. Because as he wanted to shake hands with this stern pigmy for he brought me to him, he simply stretched his hand to me before he was told that I was not the right person with whom to shake hands of course he did not put on the spectacle.

After he handed my property to the king and another pigmy put them on the ceiling and the king thanked him greatly and advised him as well to be going round the jungle every day and night and bringing all hunters or huntresses he might see in the jungle, instead to tell me to stand up, this stern pigmy simply kicked me mercilessly. As I had already rested for a few minutes, so I had gained more power and I stood up easily. Then he continued to push me along with his usual fearful big navel to their custody. It was like that my gun, hunting bag, cudgel, cutlass and the head of the wonderful animal which was dead but its eyes still had clear light, were taken from me.

As he was pushing me along to the custody thousands of pigmies were surrounded me and they were looking at me with great surprise. Not as I was a huntress but because I was taller than everyone of them. They raised up their heads and were saying—how a person was so tall as this. Because they themselves were not more than three or four feet tall. And I too bent my head downward and I was looking at each of them with great surprise that how a person was as short as this.

As he was pushing me along in the town I noticed as well that everyone of their houses was as small as a hut or not more than a room of about ten feet square and touched one another. There were many big and deep wells everywhere in the town in which they were storing their palm-oil. Everyone of them with his own family were living together in each of these small houses. But I thought within myself that they built their house so small because they themselves were so small or short.

When he pushed me to the gate of the custody, he stopped, he knocked at the door and at the same moment the sound of a cracked bell was heard. After a while the door was opened and one of the junior keepers of this custody came out. When this stern pigmy told him that the king told him (stern pigmy) to bring me to the custody, then both of them took me to the chief keeper of the custody. This chief keeper was enjoying himself with a kind of a drink at that time.

When I was first presented to him he did not talk to me or to this stern pigmy or to this junior keeper. He did not show that he saw the three of us but he was simply enjoying himself with the drink until when he finished it all and that was about two hours since when we had stood in attention before him. These two pigmies, the stern pigmy and the junior keeper, did not talk to one another at all but they stood with fear of this chief custodian or keeper.

After the chief keeper had enjoyed himself with the drink and in the mood of intoxication, he said—"Yes, what is your complaint?" Then this stern pigmy told him concisely that I was one of the hunters who were stealing away their animals from their jungle. When this chief keeper heard like that he sighed in such a way that showed me at once that he was a miscreant. And he hardly winked to this junior keeper when he ran to a big charcoal fire in which there were several flat irons. He took one flat iron from this fire. It was hot-red, and he gave it to this chief keeper as quickly as possible so that it might not cool. Then the chief keeper, without mercy, marked three big "X" on my face with this hot-red iron. When he was just marking the first "X" I felt so much pain that I started to shout greatly. When I could not stand alone in one place, the junior keeper and the stern pigmy held both my arms backward and the chief keeper marked the whole three "X" successively. This meant they gave me the mark of identification. Of course before he could give me these marks the rest two pigmies first bent my head down, because they were too short.

The Hard Life of the Custody

Cut a leave, hold it with your lips and you will see the anger of a dumb.

The house of snail is zigzag and the house of tortoise is a far jungle.

After the marks were given to me he ordered the junior keeper to take me to the right place in the custody. And he ordered this stern huge pigmy, who caught me from the jungle, to go back to the town.

Immediately this junior keeper took me to the inside of the custody, he rang a big bell for three times. At the same time about fifty junior keepers like himself rushed to him from every corner of the custody. Then after he told them my offence, he handed me to them and he went back to the chief keeper at once. These junior keepers were called "Pesters". Then one of them took me again to the room which was last to the rock. He put me among the captives whom they had captured and put in this custody many years ago.

There was no door in this room but it was surrounded by a very short wall. I saluted those whom I met in there but they answered with a very weak voice, even many of them were in a great sadness so that they could not answer me at all. When I looked at this room right round for a seat on which to sit there was none at all, and there was no mat as well, so I sat on the dirty floor which was full of pits and the smelling refuses.

After I rested for a while, then I raised up my head, I started to look at everyone's face perhaps I would see my four brothers among them, but I could not recognize them among these people at all, because the poverty had already changed their former appearances to another thing. Although I was still very young when they (my brothers) went to this Jungle of the Pigmies. The only thing which I knew about these people was that many of them understood my language, they were "yorubas". And I noticed as well that they were forty-nine in number or when I counted myself together with them we were fifty in number in this small room. Although this room did not contain the whole of us except when some of us sat on the short wall which surrounded the room.

Having waited for about one hour for these poor people perhaps they would talk to one another but they did not, then I was quite sure that they were in great punishment and sorrow. After that I went out of this room, I stood in one place, looked right round the whole of this custody and it was at this time I saw clearly that the length and breadth of it was about one-quarter of a mile square. There were more than two thousand rooms and each contained fifty captives. These captives, like myself, were hunters whom the pigmies had captured from the jungle when they came there to kill animals. Several of them had been captured since twenty years ago. The families of these hunters believed that they had been killed by the wild animals or by the pigmies when they did not return to them, not knowing that they were still alive and in the custody of the pigmies.

The wall (rock) of this custody was so high that there was no one who could climb it and escape. Even if one of us attempted to do so in the midnight he or she would be killed by the wild animals and reptiles which were on the only road which led to the town. The houses of these pesters (junior keepers of the custody) were built a little distance from the rooms of the captives. Uncountable of leather whips, dried long tails of big animals, long big bones of animals, clubs, cudgels, whips, etc., were scattered all over the ground. Uncountable of heavy lump of stones were also scattered all the ground. All these things showed me that there was nothing good in this custody but punishments upon punishments.

Almost all these captives were already naked, for all the clothes which were on their bodies when the pigmies caught them had been torn to rags. Some of those who were not so long since when they were captured still had dirty rags on bodies. They were not barbing their heads at all, so it was hardly to see their mouths, faces, ears, etc., the hairs had covered them.

As I stood in one place and I was noticing all these things and as I was just thinking in mind that in a few months to come, I too would become as dirty and in nakedness as these people or perhaps I would be killed in a few days time. There I saw a very weak man (a captive) who was running about in this custody and one of the pesters was chasing him about with a big cudgel of bone in hand. As this man was shouting with great sorrow it was so this pester was beating him with that cudgel without mercy. It was like that he was beating him until this man fell down helplessly and then died. But when I saw that he was still beating him, and as this was still a new thing or fear to me, so with pity I ran to this pester just to beg him to leave the man. But without hesitation he started to beat me on the left shoulder with great anger as when a dumb beat one who put a leave in mouth on his presence. And with much pain I ran back to my room.

Not knowing that none of the captives must do as I did otherwise he or she too would be beaten to death as well. Then I sat together with my colleagues. I began to think in mind that no doubt I would die in this custody and I trembled with fear for hours. Though several people had died on my presence before but a human like myself was not beaten to death on my presence before.

As I was a brave lady or huntress, after a little time this fear went away from my mind, but I was so hungry that if I saw a tree this time surely I would try to eat some of it because since when the stern huge pigmy had caught and brought me to this custody I had not eaten anything. As I was still thinking of my hunger, there I heard the sound of a cracked bell un-expectedly and then all the rest captives rushed out. As I was still looking on with wonder and expecting what they were going to do or what was going to happen. They were gathering together in a certain spot which was near a mighty stone. After a while there I saw some of the pesters, each of them held a basket with left hand and came to this spot. All of them were throwing a kind of fruits to the captives who were seeking these fruits along with another or picking them about and they started to eat them greedily.

Each of these fruits was as small as a palm-fruit. Not knowing that these fruits were their food for that day and this meant I would not eat till the following day. Ten minutes was given to eat the fruits. After that the whole of us were called out by the pesters. After each of them picked up one of these cudgels, club of bones, leather whips, or split of stones, etc. Then they gave the order that each of us must start to lift each of the heavy stones from one place to another. Whereas each of these stones was heavier than what four persons could even lift up.

So everyone started to take his or her own. But being I was a new captive among the rest and I did not know how to handle this heavy stone. Therefore one of the pesters who held a leather whip stood at my back and he was whipping me continuously. Within a few minutes every part of my back was bleeding. But when I saw that the blood was rushing down from my back in great quantity, willing or not I lifted up this heavy stone and I took it to the right place that the rest captives were taking their own to. And I was very lucky that it was not one of those pesters who held cudgel of bones stood at my back, otherwise he would beat me to death at once, because several of us who failed to take their own or who were too slow, were beaten to death before we closed for that day.

These pesters never wasted time, because whenever one or more of us were beaten to death, they would tell some of us to carry them and they would escort us to where they used to throw deads. The place was outside of the custody, it was near the town, because they were not burying their deads in this town.

Every year or unexpectedly a large number of us were sacrificing to their king's gods. And this was puzzled me greatly when I remembered that perhaps my four brothers were among those captives who had been sacrificed to the gods or those who had been beaten to death before I was captured. Every mistake in this custody was a great offence and the penalty was to beat the offender to death at once.

It was like that everyone of us was taking each of the heavy stones from one place to another till when it was seven o'clock. Before this time I was entirely tired. But God was so good that when I was just feeling the giddiness and I was about to fall down, the chief keeper came by that moment and he told us to close for that day. Then everyone of us hurriedly went back to his or her own room.

As a new captive who was just come to this custody,

I thought that as we went back to the rooms we would sleep till morning but it was not so at all, because as the animals like wolves, dogs, etc., and all kinds of snakes were uncountable in this custody. Therefore immediately there was darkness all over the custody, these creatures came out from their hiding places. They were going from room to room, they were looking for their food. So as we sat down sorrowfully and were resting it was so we were driving them away from us so that they might not eat or swallow us. If one was too slow to drive them away, they would eat or swallow him or her up at once or if one was napped for one second before the daybreak, these creatures would eat or swallow him or her up before he or she would wake.

It was like that the whole of us were in the trouble of these animals and snakes till five o'clock in the morning when we started our usual work. It was this night I knew that as we were in trouble in the day it was so in the night as well.

As I was in this endless punishment, it was so I was thinking in mind as how I would be able to ruin the whole of these pigmies or to see that I drive them away from this jungle. We started our usual work when it was five o'clock in the morning. The punishment which was given to me this morning was more severe than that of the first time. Because I had already tired and powerless to lift up this heavy stone as well as the first time.

When it was about eleven o'clock the chief keeper

came to us. He stopped us but before he came there several captives had been beaten to death for failing to lift up the stones as well as the pesters wanted them to do. At the same time that we were stopped by the chief keeper, halve cooked cassavas were throwing to us. But as everyone of us was running here and there just to pick up one of these cassavas before they would finish, because they were not sufficient to reach each of us, it was so the dogs, etc., were mixed up with us and they were picking up these cassavas as well. Of course I was so lucky that I did not struggle so hard when a very small one hit my head and I hastily took it otherwise several hundreds of the rest captives who had none at all would rush to me and pick it before me.

It was the same kind of this work we were doing everyday because these pigmies had no farm to take us to, and we were permanently confined to this custody except when some of us were beaten to death, then some of the rest of us would be chosen to carry the dead bodies to the place where dead bodies were throwing and that was the time when those who carried the bodies would leave this custody for a few hours.

One morning, as we had just started our daily work, the chief keeper came to us. He told us to be in fifties and in a single line and we did so at the same. Then as he was inspecting the whole of us, he was giving sign with finger to everyone that he wanted to come out from the line. So when he inspected to the line in which I was, he gave sign with finger to me to come out and I did so. We were about sixty that he told to come out. After that he ordered one of the pesters to escort us to his office which was nearest to the gate. As we stood before his office, I was saying within myself that no doubt I was going to sacrifice to the king's gods today. Because whenever some of the captives were selected as this, surely the king was going to sacrifice them to his gods.

When he came back to his office he told me to enter the office and after that he ordered two pesters to escort the rest captives to the palace of the king and they were not seen again except those two pesters who escorted them returned. He told me that as from that morning I became his office servant. He explained to me that he chose me among the rest captives simply because my clothes were clean and I was the youngest of all the rest captives. Although he did not know that I was a lady and all the pesters and the rest captives did not know as well because it were the man's clothes I wore.

My work was to clean his office and surroundings every morning and after that to be serving him with drinks because he was a pure drunkard. In a few days time when he discovered that I was smart and that I was doing everything to his entire satisfaction, he began to play and joke with me. He stopped to illtreat me as a captive again and he stopped to be fearful to me as before. And he told the pesters to be giving me sufficient food. As I started to eat enough food and I did not do hard work as before, so I became fat in a few months time.

Each time that I served him with the drink I was draining the little drink that which was remaining in the tumbler but I did not let him know or see me. Thus I was draining the drink little by little until I accustomed to the drink, and at last I was not satisfied again with the little that which was remaining in the tumbler. So whenever he went out for inspection I would drink as much as I could from his drink. As a play and as a joke I became a drunkard. But it was a pity that I had forgotten that if I drank this drink too much it would intoxicate me and by that my characteristic would be changed from when I did not drink.

As I was enjoying my life quite well in this office it was so I was thinking in mind how I could ruin these pigmies. One day, as I was going round this custody, I saw in a certain part of it a substance with which to make gun-powder. Immediately I discovered this thing it came to my mind to make a lot of native gun-powder from this substance. And having made a lot of it, then when it was in the midnight I dug several holes round the wall (rock) of this custody. I filled each of them with this gun-powder and I covered it with sand and refuses. Then I put in mind that perhaps one day the gun-powder would explode when it caught the fire and by that this custody would be blown off and then we the captives would be able to come out and then escape for our lives. It was like this I buried the gun-powder everywhere in this custody.

But it lasted me more than six months before I made enough gun-powder.

The more I was serving my master, the chief keeper, satisfactorily the more he was liking me, because after I had buried the gun-powder all over the ground of this custody I was serving him far better than before so that he might not beat me to death. But at last my joy was excessive, because as I was so careful in drinking his drink before and he did not suspect me at all, I did not do so this time, for I had already indulged myself with the drink in such a way that one morning, immediately he went out for inspection I went to the room in which his drink was kept. Then I carelessly started to drink it. But to my fear he came back to the office unexpectedly, he forgot something which he came back to take, and he met me in that room as I still put the tumbler in my mouth.

In the first instance he did not believe his eyes, then he entered the room just to make sure whether it was I. But when he entered the room and he saw clearly that I was drinking from his drink. Without hesitation he took the whole of me off the floor and he threw me from this room to the outside of the office. My head and back were so hit by the stone which was near there that I fainted at once.

Having done so he rang the bell for three times and about ten pesters came in. He ordered them to take me to the custody and beat me to death at once. But as these ten pesters were taking me to the custody it came to my mind this moment to stop to breathe entirely as if I was already dead and if I did so these ten pesters would not take any trouble to beat me but they would go and throw me to the place that they used to throw their deads and before they could do this they must carry me out of the custody and I believed that once I came out of this custody I would be able to ruin these pigmies.

Luckily when I stopped to breathe, these pesters thought that I was already dead on the way to the custody and by that they did not attempt to beat me but they told one of the captives to carry me and they escorted him to where they used to throw dead bodies and they threw me there as a dead person. After they had returned to the custody I stood up and I thanked God greatly for I came out of this custody safely, but I must not be so happy yet because I never knew whether my plan to ruin the whole of these pigmies would be successful or not.

As that place was smelling badly I hastily went to a little distance from there and I hid myself in the darkness of the cup of the rock which was the wall of this town. And again I must not go to the town at the same time or if I did so and if one or more of these pigmies saw me they would take me back to the custody and if it was so, this chief keeper would still beat me to death. That was how I came out from this custody with a trick, but the gun-powder which I had buried everywhere in this custody was not yet caught fire until when I left there. I was very lucky that this day that I left there was "The Day of Immortality" which was Sunday.

The Huntress is back to the Town and the Pigmies are in Danger

Let everyone hold his head so that the hawk of the sky may not take it (head) away.

The junction of three roads which are confusing the stranger.

As these pigmies were now in danger it was so for me as well, because if my plan did not succeed or if they overpower me it was very dangerous to me as well because they would kill me, for I would not be able to run out from their town because the wild animals, etc., which were on the road to this town would kill me as well.

I hid myself in this place for two days and I thought well how I would be able to take my gun, hunting bag, the poisonous cudgel and the wonderful head of the animal back from the palace of the king of the pigmies. After I had killed the animal the powerful light of its eyes was still alive and was still reflecting powerfully, so I had been wearing the skull of this animal as my helmet and it was helping me greatly before it had been taken from me by the pigmies.

It was later on before I remembered to be going to the town every midnight and stealing the food from their kitchens. So when it was the midnight and when I was quite sure that the whole of them had slept, I went to the town, I was entering their kitchens and I was looking for food. But I entered several kitchens without seeing food or edible thing. And as I was going from one kitchen and to another their dogs saw me and as I was too curious to them, because I was taller than their owners so they started to bark at me repeatedly.

At last when I saw that I did not see food from any of these kitchens and as I wanted to try more but these dogs wanted to suspect me to their owners, then I knelt down, I began to walk with my knees. When I did so, I became as short as a pigmy and these dogs stopped to bark at me this time as before, because I then seemed as one of the pigmies. And I searched many of their kitchens before I saw a small roasted meat which was hung near the fire. So as from that night whenever I was going to the town in the midnight I was not walking on standing again but with my knees and this persuaded these dogs that I was one of the pigmies. And I believed this night that indeed this town of the pigmies was one of the towns in which the domestic animals were surplus, perhaps the inhabitants had no teeth.

One midnight, as I was going about in this town, I came to the palace of the king in which my gun, etc., were kept when all were taken from me the other day. And as I had noticed the part of the ceiling of the palace in which all were kept the very day that I was brought from the jungle. So after I hesitated for a while and I saw that all the people in this palace had slept deeply. Then I hastily climbed this ceiling. Luckily I met all there and I took them at once. But when I came down and as I was leaving the palace I smashed a part of the king's arms and he woke at the same moment. He looked right round but he did not see me, for his eyes had already dimmed and he could not see well of course I could not say whether he was once a tailor who had been too old in tailoring work and had had no money with which to purchase a spectacle. And I was very lucky as he was in this condition or if he had the clear eyes and if he caught me there was no doubt I would be killed at once.

Immediately I came out of the palace I ran back to where I was hiding. It was like that I got all my things back.

In the following midnight I put this wonderful skull on my head as if it was an helmet, I hung my hunting bag and cutlass on my shoulder and I held the gun and the poisonous cudgel. After that I went to the centre of the town. The light of the eyes of this skull was so powerful that it was seeing everywhere in the town.

As there were several deep large wells in the centre of the town in which these pigmies were storing their oils. So I removed the covers of these wells, I gathered plenty of dried refuses and I put them in these wells. After that I put the fire in them. Having done that, I ran to the palace and I put the fire on its roof as well. Before the fire became a big flame I ran away from there and I put the fire on the roofs of several houses as well. Within a few minutes this fire had become so powerful that it spread to the whole houses. The custody caught fire as well. After a few seconds the gun-powder which I had buried in there exploded and it blown off a part of the wall. And as both captives and the pesters ran out from there to the town with great excitement the flame and the smoke of the town had risen to such a great height that the rock started to fall down heavily. Each time that it was falling down it was killing a great number of these pigmies.

When I saw that they were running here and there together with their children and with embarrassment, then with the skull on my head I started to shoot them repeatedly with my "shakabullah" gun. Whenever they saw the powerful light of this skull on my head, they were nearly fainted with fear and they would rush to another part of the town perhaps they would be saved, because they thought that I was a ghost or a cruel creature who lighted their houses with the powerful light of the eyes of this skull. As I was still shooting them continuously and as the fire was spreading more and more and the top of the rock was falling heavily to their town. They rushed to the custody perhaps they would be saved and as they were shouting greatly that they had never seen the kind of the creature who had powerful light on head, I entered the custody unexpectedly and with fear they and the captives rushed back to the town again.

As I was still chasing them about and I was killing

them, the flame and the smoke had become more powerful than ever and when the rock which was the wall of this town, could not resist the heat of the flame and smoke then it blew to the town entirely. Having seen this the captives first ran to the gate of the town. They opened the gate by force and then they ran to the jungle. But the rest of these pigmies were still hiding or loitering about because they did not want to leave the town in respect of their properties and I too did not want to leave there until when I would see the end of them. As they were still loitering about another part of the rock blew down again. It nearly to kill the rest of them, even I was lucky that this rock did not hit me because it was only a few inches to reach where I stood. Having seen this again the remaining who were not more than forty in number, rushed to the gate of the town and they escaped to the jungle. They were so confused as the "junction of three roads which are confusing the stranger" that none of them who remembered to call his family before he ran to the jungle but "held his own head so that the hawk of the sky might not take it away" which meant everyone of them tried to safe himself or herself so that I might not kill him or her.

The Kind Gorilla Saved Me
from the Debris

The farm always sees the end of farmer.
He is as ugly as the devil's cross.
The pen always sees the end of clerk.
Never you protect another person's head until
    the hawk
carries your own away.

When I saw that there was none of them remained in the town again I hastily went back to the custody with the intention to make sure that there was none of them either in the town or in the custody before I too would leave there in the morning. And when there was none of them in this ruined custody as well then I went back to the town and I rested till morning.

But unfortunately, before it was morning a part of the rock which was near this gate had blown down as well and it covered both the gate and road while I was still in the town but I did not know yet. When it was about eight o'clock in the morning, I saw clearly that there was none of these pigmies in the town except those who had already dead. After that I went to the gate just to go to the jungle. But it was a great pity, that I could not go out of this ruined town, the rock had fallen down to this gate. I tried all my best to climb this falling rock but all my efforts were in vain, after that I went back to the ruined town. And it was right as this thing happened to me because I had protected another person's head (all the captives) until when the hawk was going to carry my own head away now. Although I was very happy that I had saved all the captives but I did not know yet whether my four brothers, in respect of whom I did all these things, were among them or not.

When I went back to the ruined town I sat down confusely on one of the debris, because this day was "The Day of Confusion" which was Wednesday. When I looked round the whole town I saw that there was none of the pigmies' houses could be seen except the debris of rock. As I sat down and I was thinking how I would be able to go out, I felt to eat. Then I stood up at the same time and I went round the town perhaps I would see one of the pigmies' domestic animals which had burnt to death. But the debris did not allow me to see any. After I struggled hard in taking away some of the debris I saw that they were under the debris. So I took one big goat and I roasted the whole of it. After that I ate as much as I could from it and I kept the rest of it near the fire, but there was no water to drink because the debris had fallen on the wells which were in this ruined town.

As it was I alone remained in this town except the

sky and the ground were with me there, I was going round the bottom of the rock which was the wall of this town, perhaps I would see the way to go out at once, but there was no way at all to go out.

When it was in the night the dew was dropping down to the town and it wetted all my body so much that I started to feel much cold. When this cold was too much for me I began to look for a protected place just to keep myself safe from it, there was none at all. So having failed to get a protected place I lay on the rock, but I was unable to fall asleep because the cold of this dew was too much and the worst part of it was that it was in the harmattan wind.

In the morning, I went down from the rock on which I lay. I sat closely to the fire with which I had roasted the goat. After I warmed my body for a few minutes then I ate some of the roasted goat. Having done that I went round this ruined town again but there was no way to go out still. I raised up my head but I saw the sky through the top of the rock very far away from me. I tried to climb the rock several times but all my efforts were failed.

When it was about eleven o'clock a.m. the sun came out and its heat began to scorge me but there was no more shelter in this ruined town. It was like that I was loitering about in the debris till when the sun was set and then I went back to the fire and I began to warm myself with it after I had eaten the rest part of the goat. Thus I was in this ruined town hopelessly for about three weeks. During this period,

I was nearly killed by hunger or if I was unable to endure starvation for long time, I should had died within five days because another thing could not stay in the belly when the hunger entered it. Of course, once a while birds were mistakingly dashing in from the top of the rock and I was killing them with my "shakabullah" gun. It were these birds I was eating every day as food having roasted them, although I was longing for another kind of food badly but there was none at all.

As a play and as a joke the apron was becoming a suit, the number of the days which I was spending in this ruined town was increasing greatly, the harmattan wind was becoming more severe, the heat of the sun was becoming hotter than ever and the dead bodies of the pigmies whom I had killed were becoming bones but still there was no way for me to go out of this ruined town.

One midnight, a very powerful storm came. The noise of this storm had been hearing from the east of the jungle for a long time before it blew towards the area of this ruined town. Even when I was just hearing the powerful noise of it I thought that it was the whole of this rock wanted to fall down. So at the same moment I began to bore a part of the bottom of this rock perhaps if it was possible to do it, I would pass through there to the jungle. But all my efforts were failed at last because this rock was too thick. As I cast down near that place and as I was thinking what to do next, this powerful storm came with full force to the area of this town. Within a few minutes every part of the town was full of dried leaves and twigs which this storm brought from the jungle. As I was in the fear of the storm, these dried leaves and twigs were caught fire from the fire which was everywhere in this town. And within a few seconds this fire became a big flame. But as I was in restlessness of mind and as I was still staggering about just to safe my life there I saw that a mighty tall fruit-bearing tree fell from the top of this rock unexpectedly to the inside of this town. This tree fell down in slanting position, its branches touched the ground and its foot which had plenty of large buttresses leaned on the top of this rock.

Immediately it fell down its leaves quenched the fire which was on the spot on which it fell. Having seen it like that I ran to that spot and I climbed one of the branches of this tree. And I was very lucky that this tree fell to this town at this critical moment otherwise I would be burnt to death in a few minutes, and it was on this branch I cast down till morning. As there were many ripen big fruits on this tree, so I ate as much as I could from them. After that I began to climb it along to the top of this rock, for I thought it would be easy to do so, but I was unable to climb one-third length of it when I slipped down because it was fallen in slanting position. I tried my best to climb it to the top of this rock several times but I could not do it. When my chest and thighs were scraped off then I stopped to climb it.

The following morning, as I sat down seriously in the debris a little distance from this tree. There I saw that a number of gorillas were climbing this tree from the top of the rock down to its branches. They were coming to eat its fruits which were the most important food for them. When they climbed it to the fruits they ate as many as they could. After that they climbed the tree back to the top of the rock and from there they went back to the jungle.

When these gorillas went away and as I had noticed the way that they held the tree before they climbed it successfully. So I went back to it, I held it as the gorillas had held it and then I began to climb it along exactly as they had done, but I still failed to climb it to the top of the rock.

When I came down having failed to climb it, I sat down near it and then I was thinking in mind how to climb it successfully. After a while it came to my mind that if I could manage to tie one end of a strong rope to the neck of one of these gorillas and then to tie the other end of the rope to my waist, perhaps when that gorilla was climbing the tree back to the top of the rock so he would drag me with the rope to the top of the rock as well. Immediately this thought came to my mind I stood up with gladness and I started to look about for the rope. But unfortunately there was none. I went up and down this ruined town but there was none at all to be found. Then I came back to the tree. With my sharp cutlass I peeled plenty of the bark of this tree. I span all to a single strong rope. After that I tied my gun, the cutlass, the cudgel, hunting bag and the wonderful head together with another rope. Then

I was waiting for these gorillas to come for the fruits again, so that I might do to one of them according to my plan.

But as I was still doubting that whether they would come back to eat the fruits that day again or it would be tomorrow morning, it came to my mind suddenly that none of these gorillas would be steady until I would tie the rope on his neck. When this thought came to my mind again, my body shrank up with sadness at the same time. After a while I began to think again the way that I could tie the rope on the neck of one of them without suspicion.

Luckily these gorillas did not come again until when I remembered how I had been once setting the ropes for animals when I was in my town. Then I stood up at the same time, I went to the tree. I set one end of this rope round a big and the most attractive fruit in such a perfect way that they would not be able to see this rope at all. After that I tied the other end round my waist while my gun, etc., were on my shoulder.

It was not so long from when I hid myself under the leaves of this tree when these gorillas were climbing the tree down. Immediately they came down they scattered all over the branches of this tree and everyone of them was eating any fruit that which he saw with greediness. After a while one of them saw this fruit and he ran to it so carelessly that he did not see the rope. As he was still enjoying this fruit I pulled the rope and it strangled his neck without missing it. But he never knew yet that he was already caught in my rope. After they ate the fruits to their satisfaction then everyone of them was climbing the fruit tree back to the top of the rock. And when this one was climbing along he felt that he was heavier and it was this time he noticed that a rope was on his neck.

When the rest saw me they climbed this tree as hastily as they could with great fear. This one tried to do so but he could not, because he was then dragging me along with himself. He was trying to cut this rope as he was dragging me along but he could not cut it. When he struggled hardly for about one hour before he could drag me to the halve length of the tree, he was unable to climb it further, for he was entirely tired, so he stopped and then he was trying again to cut the rope away. And as he was turning round this tree it was so I was dangling together with my gun, etc., and I was shouting with great fear of not being fallen down and it was so this gorilla was shouting greatly as well.

Having struggled for several times to cut the rope but failed then he continued to drag me along as usual But when he nearly to climb this tree to the top of the rock he lost the control of himself and then he slipped back. He reached halve of the tree before he could stop himself. Even I was very lucky that he did not slip to the ground before he could control himself otherwise I would fall on the debris and by that I would die at the same moment.

After he rested for a few minutes then with great

noise he continued to climb along the tree, and it was so I was dangling here and there as if the rope would be cut soon. Immediately he climbed it to the top of the rock, I hastily cut the rope in the middle so that he might go away. The half of the rope was on my waist and he took away the rest half.

It was like that I came out from this ruined town, the town of the pigmies which I burnt to ashes after I had nearly killed the whole of them. When I rested for two hours on top of this rock, then I came down from it, and I went to the jungle.

From the Jungle to the Bachelors' Town

There is no another thought when the hunger enters the stomach.

Snake is hungry and tortoise is bluffing, but both tortoise and snake are food.

Compare two things which are resemble one another.

The joy of one who gives birth to a child is different from the joy of one whose child is just dead.

After I rested on top of this rock for about two hours, I came down from it and I began to travel along in the jungle. As I was travelling along it was so I was keeping watch of those pigmies who were the survivors, perhaps they were still waiting for me to kill, because as it was a great joy to me as I had ruined their town it was a great sorrow to them as their town was ruined, so by that my own joy was quite different from their own.

I did not travel so far when I was forced to stop by hunger without my wish. Because I had had no sufficient food to eat throughout the whole period that I had spent in the ruined pigmies' town, the town which was under the rock. When I stopped I looked for an animal to kill it for my food, because hunger did not allow me to decide within myself what I should do when I came back to this jungle this time, all my useful thoughts which were in my stomach escaped immediately the hunger came in. And I did not see any animal to pass this time. But when I travelled further I came across a big tortoise and a big snake. The snake was hungry and it was looking for its food. But the tortoise who was already satisfied with food, was going to and fro and it was bluffing before this hungry snake. Of course I did not see this bluffing tortoise at first except the snake. After I killed this snake and when I bent down to take it then I saw that the tortoise was there as well. And as I saw this tortoise as well I said within myself that—Oh, while I was hungry badly both of you are here when the flesh of both of you is food.

So without hesitation I picked it up as it was still going to and fro with the intention that the snake could not eat it because of its hard shells. After that I went back to the spot that I put the rest of my things. I roasted both of them with fire and I ate them to my satisfaction. I hardly satisfied my hunger when I heard the cry of a dove which reminded me that it was six o'clock evening. When I believed that it was six o'clock and that the darkness was approaching and to be able to get a suitable place to sleep, so I stood up and I began to travel along at the same time, because at the same time that I had satisfied my hunger I could decide within myself what I should do. Of course I could not travel so far when the darkness came but I used the usual "reflecting eyes" as I called it.

After a while I travelled to a big dead wood which had fallen down from a long time. I climbed it and I slept on it till morning and there was nothing happened to me throughout. Because I had nearly killed all the wild animals of this jungle before I had been captured by the stern huge pigmy.

The following morning, having eaten some ripen fruits, I continued to roam about in the jungle, I was looking for the "snake of snakes", the most fearful and dangerous boa constrictor. Before I left my town, my father had warned me very seriously about this boa constrictor, that he was one of the most danger-ous creatures of this jungle. Of course I had already killed one of the dangerous birds of this jungle, which had the voice that which was similar to that of the human being, when I was in the Ibembe town. This bird was going from this jungle to Ibembe town and it was carrying the people of that town to the jungle. It was half-bird and half-human in form.

So I was looking for this boa constrictor to be killed, because I wanted to see that I cleared up all the dangerous creatures before I would leave this jungle, so that anybody who wished to go there after I did so might go there without being killed by any dangerous creatures. But unfortunately, as I was looking about for this "snake of snakes" (boa constrictor) I did not know when I was entirely lost in this jungle. I tried my best to trace out my former track which I made before I had been captured, but I could not. Not knowing that immediately I came down from the top of that rock, I travelled to another part of this jungle instead. Anyhow, I was still travelling along and looking for him.

One morning, having taken my breakfast, I continued to travel along at once. But after a while I travelled to a river. I wondered greatly to see a big river as this in this jungle. It had very strong tides which never stopped or quiet in a moment. This river was so deep and wide that several hippopotami were swimming about on the surface of the water as they liked without any disturbance.

Immediately I came to this river, I stopped on its bank, I put all my things down and then I began to enjoy these hippopotami as they were swimming about, because I had never seen this kind of water animals in my life. As I was still looking at them with wonder they began to swim along to where the river was flowing. But as I wanted to see more about them so I left all my things on the bank of this river and I was following them with the hope to come back in a few minutes time. Unfortunately I did not follow them so far when I found myself amongst of snakes in the bush which was hung overhead near the river.

To my fear I hardly ran to a distance of about three feet when they covered me from feet to head. Although their bites could not do me anything because I had already taken the medicine which could not allow the snake-bites to affect me before I left my town. Not knowing that these snakes were living together with this dangerous boa constrictor (the snake of snakes) which I was seeking for all the while before I came to this river. His home was near the river.

But as I was still struggling with great excitement to safe myself from these snakes, I did not know that this "snake of snakes" was coming behind and he butted me unexpectedly. I fell down so heavily that these snakes were scattered to different direction with fear. But before they came back to me and as this "snake of snakes" was preparing to kill me, I hastily sprang up and I held one twig of a dead tree that which my hands reached. But as I was trying to hold this twig firmly so that I might not fall down on them and as I did not aware that this twig was already dried, so as I began to dangle to left and right, it broke suddenly and I fell into this river and without hesitation strong tides began to carry me away.

It was like that I left this jungle and my fighting weapons. I was struggling hardly to safe myself from the water but the river was very deep and its tides were too strong and unluckily I did not know how to swim. After I struggled very hardly for about twenty minutes to swim on to the bank but I failed then I left myself to death. At last the tides carried me to a part of the river where there were rocks. And as I was just sinking into the bottom of the water but the tides were still pushing me up continuously. Luckily my head hit one of these rocks and at the same moment I held the rough part of it and then I climbed it to the top. When I sat down I began to breathe quickly and audibly because I was too tired before the kind tides were pushed me there.

After two hours my mind became at rest but I was unable to go away from this rock. I stood up, I looked at my left, but this river went along without end. Then I watched whether I would see a canoe which was paddling along this time and then to beg the paddler to come and rescue me, but there was nothing on this river that which resembled a canoe. After that I looked at my back and there was nothing like a living creature on the surface of the river except the tides which were making great noises as they were hitting the rocks frequently.

At last when I did not see anyone who would rescue me from this rock which was in the middle of the river, I sat down again and I began to think with sorrow till when it was night and then I fell asleep unnoticed. And I woke suddenly from sleep when it was midnight by hunger and the noises of the hippopotami. But when I believed that if I kept longer than this on top of this rock I would die soon, the hunger would kill me. Then I sold my "death" at once, and I crept cautiously from this rock on to the back of one of those hippopotamuses. Luckily, it did not feel that anything was on its back.

After a while these hippopotami left this rock and they were finding their food to another part of the river. And it was like that they were swimming along till when it was nearly daybreak. And after a while they came to another part of this river where there was a big rock which, a part of it reached the ground. Having seen this rock, I hastily jumped from its back on to this rock and the whole of them swam away.

In the Bachelors' Town

There is no one who is rich beyond temptation.
When the front teeth fall away, the beauty of
the mouth falls.

Tiger looks at the skylark in vain. (He cannot
fly to him.)

I sat on this rock till the daybreak. This day was the "Day of Immortality" which was Sunday and I was very lucky indeed as this day was so. When I saw every part of this rock clearly then I walk on it to the forest which was near this river and I began to travel along in it at the same time. I was looking for food or fruits to eat because I was badly hungry this time. My intention was that when I satisfied my hunger then I would come back to this river, I would find my way at all costs to go back to the Jungle of the Pigmies and then to see that I killed that boa constrictor (snake of snakes) and after that to take all my things and then to go round the jungle and if I saw that there was no more any harmful creature in it, then I would find my way to go back to my town.

But to my surprise, I did not see anything which I could eat until when I was entirely lost in this forest, except those minute birds which were perching on top of every high tree, but I had nothing with me with which to kill them, and I was simply looking at them in vain as when the tigers were looking at the skylarks in vain. When I tried my best to find the way to come back to that river but all my efforts were in vain, then I left myself to the death's hand and then I began to wander about hopelessly perhaps before I would die I might reach a town or a village.

Within two days that I was wandering about in this thick forest, the thorns had torn my clothes to rags, burrs were so covered my head that my hairs were not seen again except these burrs. The skin of my legs and arms were nearly finished for the thorns which were scratching them as I was going along. Because this forest was so thick that it was hardly for a person to travel even one mile in it for twenty hours. And the worst of it was that I had no cutlass with which to be clearing my way as I was going along in it.

When it was fourth day that I had started to wander about in this forest, I came to a part of it where there was a fruit-tree. The fruits of this tree were very long and very fleshy. Of course I was not quite sure whether they were not poisonous for eating but anyhow, as I was already powerless in respect of hunger before I travelled to this tree. So I did not mind whether the fruits were poisonous or not before I began to eat those which had fallen down. After I ate them to my satisfaction, then I looked at my body but I saw that I was already half naked for the thorns which had torn my clothes to rags. Again when I touched my head the burrs were so covered it that except the whole hairs of it were cleared away before these burrs could come out.

But as I was still checking every part of my body, which was so rough and dirty that if somebody saw me that time would fear that I was insane, I heard that several cocks were crowing loudly from a long distance. When I heard like that I stood up and I began to travel to that direction at the same moment, for I believed that a town or a village must be near there.

Within one hour I travelled to one big town unexpectedly. And to my surprise was that immediately I came to this town thousands of young and old men rushed to me when they saw that I was a lady. I was first ashamed of my rough and dirty appearance when these people embraced me. But when each of them held me in a lovely way and wanted to take me to his house, then I was not ashamed again. But when I began to shout greatly for pain when my arms were about to tear away as they were scrambling me very greedily, so those old men who were scrambling me as well told the young men that the whole of them must leave me alone and the whole of them did so at the same time. After that they were arguing between themselves who would take me among them as his wife.

But when I heard the word of wife from them it revealed to me that each of them wanted me to be his wife. And as they were still arguing between

123

themselves many young men ran back to their houses, they brought food and they gave it to me to eat it. Each of them gave the food to me in such a charming way so that I might agree to choose him as my husband. Having argued for a few minutes then they arranged between themselves that they must give me chance to choose one of them for myself whom I wished to be my husband, and then they set themselves in a single line. So after I finished with the food, I started to inspect them. But as my intention was only to find my way back to the Jungle of the Pigmies at all costs. So with a trick, I simply chose an old man who was among them. This old man was so old and weary that he could not even distinguish man from woman.

It was a great disappointment and surprise for the rest people when I chose this old man instead of a young man. Of course, when the rest did not allow me to follow him to his house, his family held my arm. But as they were about to be taking me along to his house the rest started to beat them. After a while a very serious fight started. They were beating themselves with whatever they picked from the ground. At last when several people were wounded and several fell down helplessly, then they stopped to beat one another, but they took me to the palace of their king who had just died a few months ago before I came there.

After this palace was beautifully redecorated and after their king-makers cleared the whole hairs of my head together with the burrs, they took all the rags which were on my body away and after I bathed.

They gave me many costly big clothes to wear. After I dressed in these costly clothes, they put the throne at the outside of the palace. They told me to sit on it and many costly clothes were also spread on the ground on which I rested my feet. Having done that and in the presence of the whole people of this town, these king-makers put the crown on my head and then they pronounced loudly that as from this day I became their queen and that I was their ruler and to be punished one who disobeyed me.

After this ceremony was performed, the king-makers took me to the palace while the rest people were beating drums and drinking all kinds of drinks which were specially provided in respect of this ceremony.

When I sat in the palace I could not talk for two hours because when I looked at my surroundings and saw how they were beautifully decorated I wondered greatly how I came to this luxurious position unexpectedly.

When it was eight o'clock in the night, these king-makers wrapped the hairs and burrs which they had cleared away from my head before they installed me their queen, with the rags (my clothes which were torn to rags by thorns) which they had removed from my body. They wrapped the hairs and the burrs with these rags in form of a round parcel. Having done that before me then they took this parcel to a certain part of this palace. But when they returned after a few minutes, I did not see the parcel with them except one big key which one of them held. When they came back with only this key they bowed down before me and then told me to stand up and I did so at the same moment. And with a soft voice the most senior of them told me that they would be very happy if her majesty would allow them to show me the whole parts of the palace so that they might hand over the palace to me.

So when I stood up they came to my back and then I was following one of them who held a powerful light which reflected to every part of the ground on which I was smashing. They showed me every part of this palace and they repeated it that it blonged to me as from that night. But when they took me to a separate house, which had only one very big room, they showed me this key. After they warned me very seriously, that although this one roomed house blonged to me as well but I must not attempt to open the door of it because it was forbidden for me to see what was inside it. Then they gave me the key and told me to keep it with me. After that they took me back to the throne. After we dined and drank together they went back to their houses while the servants, etc., were with me in the palace.

I wondered greatly when they warned me that I must not open this room and they gave me the key of it to be kept in my possession. And I did not know what they did with my hairs, burrs and my rags which they took away from my body but all I could say was that I only saw them when they wrapped the hairs and the burrs with my rags in form of a round parcel and then took this parcel to the direction of this one roomed house. It was like that I became the queen of these bachelors.

It was after two weeks that I was in this palace as a queen before I noticed that there was not a single woman or female in this town except men or males. And it was this time it revealed to me that no wonder, immediately I came there everyone of them had wanted to marry me. I noticed as well that more than ninety per cent of the people of this 'Bachelors' town' were very rich but yet none of the ladies agreed to marry any one of them. And it was a great wonder to me when I found out later, that it was their first generation who had offended their creator who had cursed them that none of the females who would agree to marry either one of them for ever.

Of course a lot of them were musicians and for this, mighty beautiful halls were seen everywhere in the town. But I was very surprised too that as they had no wives they were still happy always. They were always dancing, drinking, beating drums and joking with one another. They were not quarrelling with each other so much. But the noises of their drums and the cheerful noises of the merrymakers were too much in this town. And for the whole period that I spent there as their queen, the merrymakers and drummers did not let me enjoy my life as luxuriously as it must be. Because they used to visit me several times a day. Whenever these visitors saw me several of them would not aware when they would open mouths widely and utter—"Ah! this is a lady whom we are longing for to marry!" Whenever they uttered carelessly like that those valets or servants were warning them at the same time not to say so and that they must remember that I was their queen.

Within a few months that I was in this happiness my mind was about to change not to go back to the Jungle of the Pigmies or my town again. It was even coming to my mind once a while that I had been a huntress before or in my life, because I was not suffered for anything and I was so much admired by these bachelors that several special concerts and many other amusements were performing each week in respect of me. But I was always afraid greatly that I was only a lady among several thousands of these bachelors whenever I was at the concerts, etc.

But when I completed about six months in this "Bachelors' town" one fine morning, after I ate nice breakfast, I drank and I wore several costly garments and after I put costly gold beads in my neck, wrists and I put earrings on my ears. Then I thought within myself that why should I not open this one roomed house which these king-makers had warned me for not to open, when the key of it was given to me and again I was the ruler of this town. After I sat down and thought in my mind like that for a few minutes, I stood up, I went to where I kept the key of this room since the day that they had given it to me. I took it and I came back to my seat. When I sat down I continued to think over about this locked room. As I was think-ing about it, it was so I was throwing this key up and catching it again as if I was simply playing with it.

At last I said within myself that the more I was the ruler of this town there was no reason why I should not know the whole secrets which were in this palace. And then without hesitation, I stood up and I went direct to this locked room. As I stood before the door I reminded myself that the king-makers had already warned me seriously the other night that I must not attempt to open the room because it was forbidden to me to see what was inside it. When I reminded myself like that I feared greatly and I moved my body just to go back to my seat. But as I was about to go back it came to my mind again this moment that as I was the ruler I supposed to know all the secrets which were in the palace. So without hesitation I put this key in the lock of this room and I hardly turned it round when the door opened.

When I entered this room with great fear, I trav-elled slowly to a part of it where there was darkness and then I stopped when I did not see anything in it. But as I began to scorn those king-makers that why had they warned me not to open this room when there was nothing in it, there I saw one bird which held the parcel (my hairs, burrs and my rags with which the king-makers wrapped the two things) with its beak. As I was still looking at this bird in the darkness with embarrassment. It flew suddenly to me and put this parcel on my head and at the same moment it flew back to the darkness and vanished immediately.

But immediately I touched this parcel with my hands with hatred just to push it away from my head, it was in the heart of big thick forest I found myself again. And when I opened my eyes and I looked at my body, I saw that I was in my usual rags. When I touched my head it was full of long dirty hairs which were twisted with the burrs and my body was as rough and as scratch as before I had been a queen.

As this was still just a dream for me, so I went to a tree which was near by. I leaned my back on it and I began to think over and over whether it was not myself who came back to this poor condition unexpectedly. And as it was a great sorrow to me immediately I found out my mistake, of course "there is no one Who is rich beyond temptation". So I blamed myself that if I had not opened that room as the king-makers had warned me not to do, I should had not come back to this my former poor condition.

As I was still blaming myself like that I did not know when I cast down under this tree and I was weeping bitterly. After a few minutes a number of pig-mies heard my voice and they came to that spot just to see who was weeping there. And I wondered greatly that immediately they saw me there that I was the very huntress who had ruined their town, they wanted to catch me for killing. But before they could do so, and immediately I saw them that they were pigmies I sprang up and I was running furiously along in this endless forest. Because I believed that they were those pigmies who had escaped when I ruined their town and nearly killed the whole of them some time ago, and they wanted to revenge of what I had done to the rest of them.

As I was running away for my life it was so they were chasing me to catch and kill. They were still chasing me along until when I saw a small hut which was in the heart of this forest. Immediately I saw this hut, I was running to it. But when they about to catch me I shouted greatly to the inhabitant of this hut to help me. And to my surprise, I hardly shouted when a very old and weary man ran out from the hut and he was asking me—"What is that! What is that!" until when he saw these pigmies at my back. Immediately he saw them that they wanted to kill me, he gave me chance to run to his hut, but he hastily expanded both his hands to left and right which were disturbed them, he did not allow them to enter his hut.

When he stopped them he asked from them what was the matter. And they explained to him with great anger that I was the huntress who had driven them out of their town after I had killed the rest of them. They told him as well that as they saw me this day they were prepared to kill me as a revenge. And they did not let this old man say anything when they forced their way in and he followed them at the same time. But I had passed to the forest through the back door of the hut as they were still explaining to him all what I had done to them some time ago.

When they searched this hut and they did not see

me from there. They told this old man to find me out at all costs. But when he refused to do so, because he wanted to safe me, then they began to beat him with the sticks which were in their hands. At last when he felt much pain he took his cutlass and he was cutting everyone of them without mercy. And when he nearly killed all of them then the rest who were not more than two or three in number, escaped. After the rest were escaped I came back to the hut, I thanked greatly from this old man. After that both of us buried those whom he killed. And that was how I came out from the "Bachelors' town".

After we buried them near his hut he gave me food and I ate the whole of it within a few seconds because I was very hungry before I came there. Although this food was not as nice as the kind which I had been eating when I was the queen of the "Bachelors' town". Having finished the food and I rested to my satisfaction, I told him that I would be living with him for some days before I would continue to find my way to go back to the Jungle of the Pigmies and he agreed.

This old man was so quiet and wise that I followed all the advices which he used to give everyday. But I was unable to look at his face or mouth whenever he was advising me, it was a great fear for me, because "When the front teeth fall away, the beauty of the mouth falls" and that was so for this old man, all his front teeth had fallen away and it made his face so ugly that it was very fearful to see always.

The fifth day, which was "The Day of three Resolutions" which was Saturday, that I was living with him and as we were discussing together how he came to live in the forest, there entered the hut a wonderful man. Immediately he entered the hut we raised up our heads and then we were expecting what he was going to say. But instead to tell us what he wanted he simply took one stool, he sat on it and then he asked for food without hesitation. Of course as this old man was quiet and wise he gave him food and water without any question.

As this wonderful man was eating he began to tell the old man that he would be living with him and he would be working for him. He told him further that his mother had wilfully thrown him in the jungle since when he was about nine years old, because he had troubled her too much. After he explained to this old man like that he (old man) asked from him his age and he replied that he was about fifty years of age. The reason why this old man asked for his age was that his voice was sharper or older than his appearance.

Both of us bursted into a great laughter when he said that he was about fifty years of age. Because we wondered greatly when we saw his height which was not more than two feet and he was so thin that I could compare him with a stick which its diameter was not more than four inches.

He was a talkative because he could talk throughout the day and night without a break and he was talking very fastly yet his voice was very sharp. He was so troublesome that he could not live with anyone but we did not aware of that at first. Whenever he was talking fastly thus he would be closing and opening his small eyes and thus he would be turning his head here and there and also sniffing the smell of that place. However, this old man pitied his condition and he agreed to him to be living with us. But when he asked for his name the following day that he came to live with us, for he (old man) had forgotten to ask for it before this time. He told us that his name was Ajantala, but the old man chuckled suspiciously and he did not say anything.

In the following morning, when this old man was preparing to go to his farm to fetch for our food, Ajantala told him that he would follow him and he agreed. But when he put some yams and some edible fruits in the basket and he asked Ajantala to carry it to the hut. To his fear, Ajantala shouted on him without hesitation—"What do you tell me to carry, old man?" and the old man repeated what he had told him to do. Again Ajantala shouted on him—"Oh, is that how you want to treat me? All right, I will teach you a sense now!" So without hesitation, Ajantala threw a handful dust into the old man's eyes unexpectedly, and as he was staggering about for help, Ajantala hit his head again with a heavy stone and then he fell down helplessly at the same time. But when Ajantala saw him in this condition he let him there and he ran back to the hut, for he thought he would die after a few minutes.

Immediately Ajantala entered the hut and met me as I was still preparing our food. With his usual sharp voice, he told me that the old man sent him to come and collect all his (old man's property) property and bring them to him, because the old man did not want to come back to his hut any more. When I first heard like that from him, I was greatly shocked at the same moment. I thought within myself that which meant this old man wanted to leave I alone in this hut and again I thought that perhaps the rest pigmies had made arrangement with him and he had agreed to them to come and kill me and perhaps that was the reason why he wanted to leave his hut without me.

As I was still suggesting in mind like that, Ajantala had put the whole of this old man's property at the front of the hut. Not knowing that when the old man lay down in the pool of blood for a few minutes he got up and then he was coming back to his hut when the blood stopped. But when he met Ajantala as he was just tieing all his property into one bundle and after that to carry them away, he challenged him at the same time that what was he doing with his property. Of course Ajantala did not deny at all, he explained to him that he was going to sell them. When he heard like that from him he began to struggle with him to take them back from him while I stood near the hut and I was looking at them.

But at last when I believed that Ajantala wanted to overpower him and if it was so, he would run away with the property. So I ran to them and I helped the old man to take his property back from him. But Ajantala held the property so tightly that we could not take it from him till this old man became dizzy and then fell down, because too much of blood had run down from his forehead when Ajantala hit the forehead with a stone in the farm.

Now it remained I alone who was ingrafting Ajantala not to take this bundle (the old man's property) away. Although I was a brave huntress but I was unable to conquer Ajantala at all. Because as he was so small and thin he was very strong like a giant. After a while he flung me away as if I were a grain of maize, but I hastily gripped his thin legs when he was about to run away with this bundle. But as he was trying to take his legs back from me he fell down. Now both of us held ourselves and we were beating ourselves mercilessly while he still held the bundle with his left hand. Luckily when he was about to overpower me the old man stood up. He came to us, he ran to Ajantala's back, he snatched the bundle from him unexpectedly and then he ran to the hut with it while Ajantala was still beating me and I was beating him as well.

This old man hardly kept the bundle in the hut when he ran back to us when he believed that Ajantala would beat me to death soon. Then both of us were now beating Ajantala until when we were tired. When Ajantala stood up he ran to the hut, he searched it but he could not trace out this bundle because the old man, the owner of it, hid it under a big pot but Ajantala did not remember to open it. When he failed to trace it out, we thought he would go away. But when he did not go away, this old man told him frankly that he did not want to see him in his hut any more. But to our fear, Ajantala replied that he would not go away except when he got the bundle back. At last when the old man failed to drive him away from his hut he left him. But he was still troubling us badly to take this bundle away and whenever we were eating he would eat it along with us without asking him to do so.

It was when Ajantala was trying to steal this old man's property (bundle) away it revealed to him that Ajantala was one of "The forest burglars". As he was living with us without the wish of this old man, it was so he was searching everywhere perhaps he would be able to trace out the bundle.

At last when he failed to trace it out he began to pull the roof of this hut down little by little. When the old man believed that he would pull the whole hut down in a few days time and again if we did not keep ourselves away from him this time he would kill us when we fell asleep if he could not get the bundle back. So one night, when Ajantala lay down roughly as if he had slept. This old man first suggested that the better thing to do now which could safe us from him was to pack all our blongings and leave this hut this night so that we would travel far away before he would wake in the morning.

When this old man suggested like that I supported him, I told him that it would be better now to pack our food and the rest of our blongings in a big basket and then to leave there at once. Of course I had no any blongings which I could pack except this old man. Because this time I was just as a "bird who has no property to take along with himself whenever going to somewhere except his feathers". All of my blongings were in the Jungle of the Pigmies. So at the same time I helped this old man to pack all his blongings together. I tied them together into a bundle. I put this bundle in a big basket, after that we put our food, basins, pots, etc., on top of the bundle. Having done that we hid this basket in a corner of the hut, then we went to the stream which was not so far away from there, to bathe. But not knowing that Ajantala never fall asleep when we began to make this arrangement and he heard how we were going to do.

So after we left for the stream he stood up cautiously and as he was very short and thin, he simply put all the things which were in the basket down. He went inside it, after that he put all these things on top of himself. Ajantala arranged these things so perfectly that we did not suspect that he was at the bottom of the basket when we returned from the stream.

Immediately we returned this old man helped me to put this basket on my head, after that he put the bundle (his property) on his head, after that we left this hut cautiously so that Ajantala might not wake, for we thought that he was still sleeping, although we did not put on the light and the hut was so dark that we hardly saw even ourselves. It was this bundle Ajantala was trying to steal away.

As we were travelling along very hastily and having

travelled about one mile away from this hut. And as we believed that we had already freed from Ajantala who was inside the basket, we began to scold and curse Ajantala badly and he was hearing all, but we did not know at all. When we travelled till daybreak, then we stopped when we felt to eat. Without fear, this old man helped me to put this basket down. After we put it down and as I was taking some plates from the basket, Ajantala jumped out from it suddenly. When we saw him jumped out this old man and I scattered to different direction unexpectedly with great fear. Because this fear was so much that we could not hesitate to see who jumped out from the basket. And it was after a few minutes before we came back to the basket and unfortunately, Ajantala had carried all of this old man's property away.

When we came back but we met only empty basket then it revealed to us that Ajantala was inside the basket as I had been carrying it about. So we took this empty basket and then we began to find him about at the same time, perhaps if we could find him out we would be able to take the property (bundle) back from him. It was like that Ajantala, the noxious burglar of the forest, stole all of this old man's property away.

But we could not travel so far when this old man became very seriously ill for his property which Ajantala had stolen away. When he could not walk again, I put him on my back and then I continued to travel along. And when I travelled until my back was paining me I put him down under a tree. I built a booth and I lay him under it, after that I covered him with broad leaves because there was no cloth to be used. After this, I went round there and luckily I did not travel so far when I came to a farm. Yams and corn were planted on one halve of this farm while a lot of big guords were planted on the rest halve part of it.

When I came to this farm the first thing which I did was that I went round it just to make sure whether the owner of it was there or not. But when I did not see anybody there, then I took some yams and corn and I took one big guord. After that I went back to the old man. When I made fire and put two yams and corn in it, then I went to the river with that guord. After I cut its head away and washed inside of it thoroughly, then I drew water with it and I brought it to the booth. After the old man and I ate the yams and the corn to our satisfaction we drank from this water to our satisfaction as well.

It was like that I was doing everyday until when this old man became well and then we continued to find Ajantala about. One morning, as we were roaming about we came to a tree in which there was a hole. Not knowing that Ajantala had foreseen us while we were still far away. And he entered the hole of this tree, he hid himself inside it and he was waiting for us perhaps we would travel to that spot. After a while we travelled to this tree. But as it had plenty of leaves which threw cool shadow on the ground and again as we were very hungry and thirsty, so we stopped under this tree. After we put our yams and corn down, I made fire at once, I roasted them. After I peeled away the backs of these yams we began to eat them. But as this old man leaned his back on this tree and as we were eating the yams greedily Ajantala stretched his hand from the hole of this tree and he pulled up the hairs of this old man's head. When he first did like that the old man was greatly shocked with fear when he felt much pain. He raised his head up, he looked at this tree but he did not see anybody there. Because Ajantala had hastily put his hand back into the hole of the tree. After a while he knocked this old man's forehead again with a stick and when he raised his head up again he did not see anything and this was a great wonder and fear to him.

It was like this Ajantala was illtreating him until when I put the water in my mouth. As I was drinking it, Ajantala stretched his hand out from the hole of this tree again and as he was still pulling up the hairs of this old man's head as before, I saw his shadow in this water. Immediately I saw the shadow of his hand in the water, I hastily looked at the tree and I saw plainly that it was his hand. Without hesitation, I gripped it and I began to pull it but he could not come out. He was only shouting for pain. As I pulled his hand but he could not come out from this hole, then this old man ran to the other side of the tree and he saw the entrance of the hole there. Then I left his hand this side and I went to the other side as well.

When I joined the old man, willing or not we pulled him out. After that we beat him until when he confessed to us where he hid the old man's property which he had stolen from us when he hid inside the basket the other day. And we went there, we collected them, but he had sold all the household utensils and some clothes. After that we continued to roam about while Ajantala still lay helplessly on the ground because we beat him too much and we believed before we left him that he would die after a few minutes. That was how we got some of this old man's property back from Ajantala.

But we did not aware that after a few days Ajantala became well and then he started to look for us just to take this old man's property from us at all costs. Of course, we did not believe that if even he became alive again he would be ever attempted to do so again.

The Rolling and Talking Guord

The style which I have never seen in my life, the son is riding the horse but his father is fetching for fodder.

One whose head coconut is broken will not be able to wait and eat it.

Immediately we took the rest of this old man's property from the place in which Ajantala hid them we continued to travel along as hastily as we could so that we might be able to find a suitable place on which to build another hut and again we feared greatly as we were carrying this old man's property about. Because we believed that there were still many "forest burglars" like Ajantala in this forest, and it was not safe still if we did not build a hut and keep the property in it in time. But we could not find out a suitable place till one day when we came to the farm from which I took yams, corn and big guord the other day when this old man was seriously ill.

When we came to this farm, I explained to this old man that it was from that farm I took yams, corn and guord when he was ill. So when we came there we took some yams, we made fire near the halve part of it on which big guords were planted. We put these yams inside the fire to be roasted. But when they were roasted enough and when we were about to start to eat them after their backs had been peeled off. There we saw unexpectedly that one of these big guords which was not so far away from us, began to roll itself on the ground towards the spot that we sat before the fire. And as we were still looking at it with great fear and embarrassment, we heard that it was singing as well, thus—"The guord is driving them away! The guord is driving them away! The guord which has no hands! The guord which has no feet! But the guord is driving them away! And if the guord can overtake them, will kill them! The guord will eat them!"

Immediately we heard this fearful song again from this guord, we began to run away for our lives. But to our surprise, as we were running away furiously it was so this guord was rolling and chasing us along. After a while this old man was feeling tiredness but I was still pushing him with hands as I was running along, so that this fearful guord might not be able to overtake us because "not one whose head a coconut is broken will wait to eat it" he would die of headache at once.

And with great fear we did not know when we ran to a distance of about two miles and this guord did not attempt to go back from us and this old man was so tired that he was going to fall down soon and I too were so tired that I was unable to be pushing him along with hand any longer this time. This rolling and talking guord was indeed "a style which I had never seen in my life", because as he was chasing us along it was so it was singing this fearful song which was so fearful to us that even if it killed us at once without singing this song it was far better.

Luckily when this old man and I were entirely powerless to be running along, we saw a river. This river was very big, wide and deep as well. Its bank was very steep. So when we saw it at a distance of about four thousand yards, we began to run to it at the same moment and to our surprise this guord was still following us. Immediately we ran to it, we hastily entered one canoe which was tied with a rope to a tree which was on the bank. We hardly cut the rope when we began to paddle it along on this river. But as the tide of this river was very strong so the canoe could not move as fast as we wanted it to move. And after a few seconds it was unable to go forward but the tide was pushing it here and there and again as we were in this fear all the property of this old man fell into the river and the tide carried them to the bank at the same time.

As the canoe was still doing so, this rolling guord was seen rolling down the steep bank and when it nearly to reach the river, it hit a rock and then broke into several pieces. To our surprise was that when this guord broke, it was Ajantala who came out from it. He stood up at the same time and he began to scold at us, he was throwing stones at us and he was laughing at us funningly. But when it revealed to us this time that it was Ajantala, who was inside the guord and who had been singing and driving us to kill all the while, we became so much angry that we started to paddle the canoe back to the bank perhaps we would be able to catch him. But alas, the strong tide did not allow the canoe to go to the bank direct, but it swerved to the direction where the tide was stronger instead.

We wondered greatly when it was Ajantala who came out from this guord when it broke. Because we did not know how he managed to enter into it and again it was a great surprise to us as he had been rolling along together with it as if it was somebody who had been pushing this guord along.

When he was quite sure that the canoe would sink if we force it to come to the bank. He picked up all of this old man's property which were scattered all over the bank and then he tied them into one bundle. But when this old man saw him as he tied them together and he was preparing to carry this bundle away. He told me that willing or not, we must force the canoe to the bank at once, so that we might take his property (bundle) back from Ajantala. But as we were forcing the canoe to go to the bank carelessly, we did not aware when it ran to the strong tide and then it sank suddenly. So he swam to where Ajantala was and I too swam to the other bank without my wish. The old man was entirely tired before he could swim to where Ajantala stood on the bank and I was entirely tired as well before I could swim to the other bank of this river where there was a jungle.

But before he got out of the water to the bank, Ajantala had carried his property away. It was like that Ajantala, the "forest burglar", stole this old man's property away for the second time. Now, I stood on the other bank, I could not swim back to him and he too could not swim to me. So we were looking at ourselves with great sorrow. At last when we did not know what to do before both of us could be together as before, I waved hands to him for a few minutes and then I bade him good-bye with sorrow and tears which were rolling down from my eyes. When he looked at me till when I disappeared in this jungle, then with great sorrow and tears, he left the bank of this river for that forest. It was like that this old man, who took great care of me as if he was my father, and I departed from one another without our wish.

Back to the Jungle of the Pigmies

The clock which strikes twelve, is coming back to strike one. And after it strikes one, it will strike half again.

Now, I came back to this Jungle of the Pigmies. The jungle which I had left without my wish when the fearful boa constrictor, the "snake of snakes", wanted to swallow me the other day. This day which I came back to it was "The Day of Immortality" which was Sunday. Immediately I discovered that it was the Jungle of the Pigmies, I was greatly shocked with fear. Because I believed that no doubt, I came back to the usual troubles. Especially when I remembered that there were no gun, cutlass, the cudgel, etc., with me with which to defend myself as before. And I did not know the real part of this jungle in which I put them before the "snake of snakes" had attacked me the other day. Although when I remembered that this day was "The Day of Immortality" I did not fear so much again. Of course there might be some troubles for me later on but there was no fear of death at all.

However, I was travelling along in this jungle confusely. And I wondered greatly that I did not travel so far from the bank of this river when I saw a rough track. Again I did not travel so far on this track when I saw about ten pigmies who were travelling on this track towards me. We saw one another at the same moment. As I had no any weapon with me with which to fight them, so I hastily picked some pebbles from the ground and after that I began to run away for my life. But as they had recognized me at the same time that I was the huntress who had ruined their town. So they began to chase me to catch. A few minutes after they scattered in the jungle so that they might be able to catch me.

When I believed that if I continued to run along like that they would catch me at all costs, so I climbed a tree to the top and I hid there. After a few minutes they travelled to this tree. They surrounded it without hesitation and then they were expecting that I would come to them soon without knowing that they were there already. Of course, they did not see me on top of this tree until after a few minutes when one of them raised his head up and he saw me on top of this tree. But when he was about to tell the rest that I was on top of the tree, I hastily threw one of the pebbles at him and it hit him on the left eye so hardly that he fell down suddenly. When the rest saw him did so they scattered away with fear, because they did not know what happened to him.

A few minutes later, they came back, but that one whom I stoned had already died. When they saw that one of them was stoned to death they became so wild at this time that they started to look at the top of every tree and inside of every hole which was in this spot. After a few seconds they saw me as I cast down on top of this tree. They hardly saw me there when one of them was greedily climbing the tree from the bottom, he was coming up to catch me. Again when he nearly to reach where I was, I threw another pebble at him and it hit his forehead. He fell down and he began to shout greatly for pain. It was so I was killing them one by one until they remained two. Having seen this again, the rest two began to stone at me continuously. But when I believed that they would stone me to death soon if I did not find my way to escape, I jumped down suddenly and before they attempted to catch me I started to run away.

Within a few minutes they caught me. After they beat me mercilessly for some minutes, they said that they would not kill me at the same time but they would take me to their new town when they would do that before the rest of their people. Then they cut slender sticks. Each of them held more than two of these sticks. After that they arranged themselves into a single line and they put me in the middle. Then after they put a very heavy stone on my head and they tied both my arms backward, we started to travel along on this track. Whenever I fell down the whole of them would beat me mercilessly with that sticks for some minutes before we would continue our journey.

After we travelled for some hours I began to feel hunger badly but they did not give me anything to eat.

Of course they were eating the ripen fruits which they were picking along this track and they were drinking water whenever we travelled to a river but they would not allow me to drink from this water at all. As we were travelling along it was so they were adding more to the load which was on my head so that it might be heavier than what I could carry. After a while, when I could no longer afford this non-beating and as the load was too heavy for me to be carrying it along any longer, I began to groan. By this time I fed up to be alive any more. At last when this sorrow was too much for me I begged them to kill me at once but they refused. They told me that they would take me to their new town and the rest of their people would see me before they would kill me.

It was like that I was still groaning along this track till we came to the place that they were living at about six o'clock in the evening. The place which these pigmies lived this time was in the crevice of the rock which was in a dark part of this jungle. The place was so dark that if they themselves did not follow me I would not know that they were living in there.

When we travelled further in this crevice of the rock we came to a part of it which was flat and there was light and that was their new town. Before we came to that place they nearly beat me to death because I fell down several times.

Immediately the rest of them saw me they came and were surrounded me. After those who caught me explained to them how they caught me and they explained to them as well that I had killed a number of them before they could catch me. Everyone of them began to push my nose with fingers and was saying—"Yes, she is this. She is the very lady who had nearly killed the whole of us before she ruined our former town." As they were pushing my nose and mouth with their fingers, the heavy stones which were on my head fell down and they hit one of them who died after a few minutes. Having seen this again, the rest became more angry than ever. And then the whole of them beat me to their satisfaction before they tied me to a tree. After they tied me to this tree with a strong rope with the hope to kill me the following morning, they went back to their houses. Of course it was this time it revealed to me that these pigmies were still living in this jungle, although they were not more than two hundred in number.

As I was tied down there it was so I was thinking in mind how I would cut the rope so that I might be escaped before the following morning. Because if I failed to do so before the morning, no doubt these pigmies would kill me. After a while it came to my mind to be biting a part of this rope little by little until when it would be cut into two. So I kept this plan in my mind. And when I believed that they had slept then I began to bite a part of it. But it was about two hours before I could cut it because it was very strong and thick.

After I cut it to two I tried to loose the half of it which was in my neck away but I could not do it.

When I believed that if I continued to do so, I would not be able to loose it away until the morning then I started to go away cautiously while the remaining of this rope was still in my neck. But when I was about to leave there their dogs woke from sleep and they were barking at me repeatedly.

As I was still going along in this clumsy rock these pigmies woke when they heard that their dogs were barking. When they went to that tree and they did not see me there, they started to chase me at the same time. But as they had already accustomed to travel in a clumsy crevice of the rock as this one, so I was unable to go far before they saw me at a little distance from them. But they could not catch me till I came out from this rough rock entirely and then I hastily climbed to the top of a tree, I hid myself there.

After a while they rushed out to the jungle, they were going here and there perhaps they might see me but they did not see me. After they passed through this tree to another part of the jungle, I looked at every part of the jungle but it was very dark. After I thought in mind to which part of it should I travel so that these pigmies might not see me and I never knew yet. It came to my mind suddenly that probably they might see me on top of this tree when they were coming back. So I hastily came down from it and at the same time I began to travel cautiously along to another part of the jungle. Although I could not travel so fast for both fear and hunger had forced me to become mad.

As I was going along, whenever I heard the noise made by the collision of two trees, etc., I would be startled at the same time and I would lie down for some minutes before I would continue to go along because I thought these pigmies were coming to that direction. And it was so I was dashing to trees and stumps or rocks several times but for the fear of these pigmies I would not be able to wait and take care of myself.

As I was still going along zigzag in this darkness, I travelled to a spot, the small plants of this spot were shaking. Having seen it like that I stopped and I lay down quietly. I thought it were the pigmies who were coming to me. But at last I saw that it were two snakes who were fighting on this spot. Although it was midnight this time, I could not see them clearly so that I might tell their names but as they were shaking every plant of this spot showed me that they were big snakes. As I lay down before them quietly and with great fear so that they might not attempt to bite me, I was waiting for them to go away and then to continue to go along. But instead to go away they were still fighting and biting themselves until when they were tired. I believe that this would be a great surprise to hear that I as a huntress feared to approach snakes. Yes, it must be so, because when there are no gun-powder and shots the gun becomes a mere stick. All my fighting weapons were still on the place which I put them before I was attacked by the "snake of snakes" the other day.

When I saw that they were tired I took one heavy stone and I beat them to death with it. Then I held both of them and I continued to go along. When I travelled further, I stopped, I sat down on a big dried wood, and as I was resting it was so I was thinking of the past troubles, how the present would be, how the future would be and how I would be able to get fire with which to roast these two snakes before I would eat them. As I was still thinking in mind like that I did not know when I fell asleep after I loosened the rest rope away from my neck. And before I woke it was in the morning. I could not say what woke me, whether it was the hunger or the heat of the sun which had already shone to everywhere.

After a while, as I still lay down on this wood, I felt pain of hunger in my stomach. This pain was so much that I must turn my left loin to the right. When I did so, there I saw that a very big snake was already puckered closely to my head and several coiled round the trees which were near me and uncountable of them lay on the ground before me as well. All of them raised their heads up and they were looking at my eyes as if they were told to be keeping watch of me so that I might not run away or to stand up from this wood. But I believed that if I dare attempted to stand up and run away for my life they would bite me. Even I had no more power to run or to fight with any creature this time. And to my fear the biggest one of these snakes lay on a part of my cloth and I was so feared that I could not pull the cloth away from it. Of course it revealed to me after a while that this area was the home of the snakes and all kinds of the reptiles.

As I lay down, on this wood and as they were looking at me very fearfully, I began to sweat and I was trembling with great fear of not being killed by them. Especially the biggest one of them which puckered very closely to my head and fixed its eyes staringly at me. But at last when they did not attempt to go away and again it came to my mind this moment that perhaps these pigmies were still looking for me and perhaps they would come to this area soon. So without hesitation I sprang up and then I began to run away for my life while I still held those two snakes which I had killed in the night before I came to this spot. As I sprang up and I began to run away, these snakes scattered at the same time and they were ready to bite me. But when they saw that I was running away from them they were chasing me along.

I was greatly surprised and feared that as I was climbing the hills and rocks just to hide myself from them it was so they were following me and were driving me away from there. Whenever I climbed a tree they too would climb it and without hesitation I would come down when they were about to bite me. It was like that these snakes were still chasing me about until when I was tired. But as they did not go back from me in time, I ran to the bank of the river on which I put my gun, cutlass, hunting bag, etc. before I was attacked by the "snake of snakes" the other day. And I did not run so far on this bank when I ran to where I put them. Without hesitation I took the cutlass and the poisonous cudgel and I began to beat these snakes to death. Within a few minutes I nearly killed the whole of them. Having seen this the rest of them which still coiled round my body ran away. It was after I freed from them it revealed to me that they attacked me in respect of two of them which I had killed in the night.

Then I went back to where I put the rest of my things. I took them, after that I went round there and I found a big hole which was under a big rock. I swept all the refuses which were inside it away. I put all my things in it. After that I made fire and I roasted those two snakes and I ate some of them at the same time. Having rested for a few minutes, I checked all my things and they were correct. But the gun-powder which was inside the gun before I left the jungle, was already wet together with the chamber of the gun. So I washed the chamber with water and within one hour that I hung it near the fire, it was dried. Then I loaded it with new gun-powder and shots and then I was waiting perhaps those pigmies would come so that I might shoot them to death, because I did not fear them again for I had got my fighting weapons.

It was like that I found out my usual "shakabullah" gun, etc. But the following morning, I took my gun, etc., and then I began to find the fearful boa constrictor ("snake of snakes") about. It was this "snake of snakes" had attacked me the other day. After I travelled for a while I came to the same spot that which he was when he attacked me the other day. But I did not see him immediately I came to this spot. And as I wanted to kill him at all costs this morning, so I began to find him about. After a while I travelled to a big rock which was near the river which had been carried me away the day that he attacked me. There was a huge hole under this rock. The hole of this rock was through to the river. And as the refuses which were at the entrance of it were parted to both sides, I believed that it was his home.

I stood before this entrance and I was thinking whether to enter the hole or to wait at the outside till when he would come out by himself. Of course I entered it when my mind told me to do so. I travelled to left and right of it but I did not see him. Although the darkness which was in a part of it gave me a doubtful mind that he was in there. At last when I did not see him, I sat down and I was waiting for him perhaps if he was in that darkness he would come out after a few minutes time.

Not knowing that he was not inside the hole at that time but he had gone to the river through the other entrance of the hole. After a while he came in back with his body which was still wet with water. Immediately I saw him I stood up, and I held my gun ready. And he too hardly entered the hole when he was preparing to jump upon me and after that to swallow the whole of me because he was then hungry badly.

When I noticed that he wanted to do so, I hastily shot him at head but this was only lessened his power and could not prevent him from coming to me. When he jumped upon me and before I could do anything again he had coiled round my body and within this moment he pushed me down. Having seen this, I did not attempt to fire at him or to beat him with the poisonous cudgel but I left myself to him. But as he could not swallow me because I had shot him at head, he was just rubbing me against the ground which was so swampy that I nearly sank into the mud before I fired at his throat.

Immediately the gun-shots hit his throat he sprang to a short distance and before he could do anything to me again, I ran to him and I began to beat him with the poisonous cudgel. All the blood which was gushing out from his body was so spilling upon me in large quantity that I was entirely wetted with it. As I was beating him with this cudgel and he did not die in time, then I began to cut every part of his body with cutlass. This critical moment he became so wild that he was dashing to every part of the hole with the hope to hit me to death and it was so I was cutting him repeatedly. After a while we made this hole so rough that we did not know when we came out.

But after I wounded him very severely, and the blood which gushed out from his body was too excessive, then he fell down and he died. So it was like that I saw the end of this boa constrictor, the "snake of snakes". And he was powerful and fearful as my father had told me before I left my town for this jungle.

After I killed him, I went back to his hole, I picked

up my gun and the poisonous cudgel from the place on which they had scattered, and then I came out and I went back to my hole with gladness. When I returned to my hole, I put my gun, cutlass and the cudgel down, I went to the river and I washed the blood and the mud away from my body and after that I took all the refuses away from my hair. When I came back I ate some of the roasted snakes and after that I rested till the evening.

In the evening, I went out, I picked some fruits and I killed one small porcupine on my way coming back. I ate some of these fruits and some of this porcupine having roasted it. After that I closed the entrance of this hole before I slept so that a dangerous animal, etc., might not come in to me. But the following day, when I waited till the evening for these pigmies and they did not come to me. Perhaps they were still finding me about I could not say. So when it was midnight, I took my gun, hunting bag, cutlass, the poisonous cudgel and I put the "reflecting eyes" on my head and then I started to go to their new town which was in the crevice of the rock.

As I was going along the light of this "reflecting eyes" reflected to my front to the distance of about one mile. When I travelled near their town, I covered these "reflecting eyes" so that these pigmies might not wake until I would travel to the centre of their town. Having travelled to the centre of their town, I first shot at one of them before I took away the cover of these "reflecting eyes". When the powerful light of these "eyes" reflected to every part of their town suddenly, they rushed out from their houses with great confusion.

And as they were hustling here and there with embarrassment just to go out from there to the jungle, I ran to the road on which they would travel. I began to shoot them to death. After a while the rest went back to the town and I was following them and it was so I was shooting at them.

After a few minutes, when I did not see them again, I thought I had killed the whole of them. But not at all, it remained one of them who hid himself somewhere in the town. This one was the most dangerous and powerful of all. When it was daybreak and as I believed that no doubt I had killed the whole of them, I began to go round there. But to my fear there I saw that this one was coming to jump upon me. Having seen him coming like that I hastily squatted and he fell on my head. Without hesitation I stood upright and then I knocked his back against a rock with the hope that he would die at once. He became dizzy for a few seconds only instead. But when he sprang up with the hope to press me down, I dodged to my right and he fell on the ground. Before he stood up again I beat him with the cudgel. But as I was beating him with greediness so I did not know when I beat my left knee and then I fell down at the same moment. Before I could stand up he ran to me and he sat on my belly and then he was beating me on the face, etc. Of course when I struggled hardly for a few minutes I turned somersault. As he was now under my belly, so I pressed him hardly against the ground before I began to beat him with a piece of flat stone.

But when he felt much pain he kicked my belly with both his feet and I sprang far away from him. And as I was just standing up he ran to me and he gave me several blows in the face and jaws. But as I was skipping to left and right and to front and back, just to defend myself and as he was trying to get me round with the hope that he was going to conquer me very soon. So I butted his belly with my head suddenly and without hesitation I carried the whole of him up and then I knocked him against the rock which was nearby. His head and back hit the rock so hard that he fainted at the same time. And he was still in this condition when I ran to my poisonous cudgel. I picked it up and I beat him to death at once.

After I rested for a few minutes I went round this town perhaps these pigmies were still remained alive, but when there was none of them who was alive then I took some of their yams and I came back to my hole at the same time with gladness. It was like that I killed the whole generation of these pigmies who had killed and detained several thousands of hunters who had come to hunt, etc., in this fearful jungle. Of course I never knew yet whether my four brothers, in respect of whom I came to this Jungle of the Pigmies, were alive or the pigmies had killed them.

I was so happy this day that I killed all the rest of these pigmies that the following day I killed a big bush-goat. After I washed my "shakabullah" gun, cutlass, and the poisonous cudgel as well. Then I gathered them together under a tree which was at the front of my hole and I soaked them with the blood of this bush-goat for they had helped me greatly to conquer my enemies, because "one who lives on band or drum must take care of leather." So after I ate some of the flesh of this bush-goat I remained in this hole happily throughout this day. I did not go out to the jungle at all.

Good-bye to the Jungle of the Pigmies

Hastily, hastily, hastily, the sun is going back to its place of yesterday.

The following morning, I put my hunting bag, gun, and cutlass on the shoulder. I held the poisonous cudgel and after I kept this wonderful "reflecting eyes" in a corner of this hole, then I began to go round this jungle, just to make sure that there was no more dangerous creature in it. And I was killing all the wild animals which I was meeting on the way. It was so I killed the whole of them. It was even hardly to see any of those harmless animals, as antelopes, etc., this time. After that I came back to my hole.

But one morning, when I was looking about for edible fruits I came across a number of those hunters whom I had saved out of the pigmies' custody. When they first saw me they wanted to run away, because they thought that I was one of the pigmies. But when I waved hand to them not to run away, they stood quietly with great fear in one spot. When I travelled to them I explained to them that I was the very huntress who had saved them out of the custody the other day. They were so wondered and happy when they heard this from me that they embraced me and then took me to where the rest of them hid.

When I counted the whole of them they were more than four hundred. They told me that abundant of them had returned to their respective towns immediately they came out from the custody, but they remained in the jungle as they could not trace out the right way on which they could travel back to their own town. When they explained to me like that with gladness, then I told them the name of my town and the name of my father and I asked from them whether anyone of them knew my father or mother. I gave them this description so that I might know whether my four brothers were with them or not. But to my surprise I hardly described myself like that when my four brothers ran to me and they embraced me and I did so as well.

I explained to them further that I had fought with the whole powerful creatures and I had killed the whole pigmies of this jungle. I told them as well that I had been to the "Bachelors' Town", in which I became a queen. After these explanations, I told the whole of them to follow me back to my hole. So everyone of them took his blongings and they followed me at once.

We built a number of temporary booths at the front of my hole. They were living inside them while I was living inside this hole as their leader. But when I believed that it would be easier for us to travel by river than by land because everyone of them was too weak to trek a long distance. So the following day, after we took breakfast, we began to cut down mighty trees which we were going to carve into canoes. Although it took us several weeks before we made sufficient canoes because we had no other instruments except my cutlass. After we constructed sufficient canoes and pushed them to the bank of the river, then I began to kill animals like deers, antelopes, bush-goats, etc. We were eating their flesh while I was putting their skins in the sun to dry. Within two weeks I killed more than one thousand animals. When we were unable to finish their flesh as before, then we roasted them with fire while their skins were hung in the sun to be dried. Of course these people and my four brothers never knew yet what I was going to do with these skins.

When I believed that I had got sufficient skins and roasted meat, then with the help of these men I dug plenty of gold dust, silver, copper, brass, antimony, etc., etc., etc., because all these precious metals were very common in this jungle. After that we put them in one of the canoes. But when we were ready to leave this jungle in the following morning. The whole of us were going about in this jungle, we were fetching for the edible fruits which we would be eating together with the roasted meat along the way to my town. After a while we came to a curious fruit-tree. It was so curious that we did not know the name of it. Each of its fruits was as small as a chocolate and a part of it was as creamy and cold as ice. Having tasted it, it was as sweet as a chocolate and that part of it was just as ice-cream. So for this reason we plucked uncountable of them and we put them in one of the canoes as well.

We woke up very early in the morning, I gave each of the skins to each of these men to wear it, because everyone of them was already naked and it would be a great shame to them if they appear to the town in this shameful condition. After each of them wore the skin and we ate to our satisfaction, then we went to the river. After I nailed the "reflecting eyes" on the front of the canoe on which I was going to sit. For we were going to use this "reflecting eyes" as our lamp.

This "reflecting eyes" as I called it, was the head of the fearful animal which had sixteen long and sharp horns and which I had fought with and killed long ago. After it was dead its eyes which were in its skull did not die but both were still reflecting very power-fully like a powerful light. Having nailed this wonder-ful skull or "reflecting eyes" on the front of the canoe then we pushed the whole of the canoes on the river. My own canoe was at the front while the rest were at back, and a number of men who would be paddling it sat in it with me.

As this day was "The Day of Victory" which was Tuesday and as we wanted to be in my town before coming Tuesday. So each of these men took one of these curious fruits and put it in his mouth. As they were eating them at a time they formed a kind of a song. They first shouted greatly with great joy just to show that they were leaving this jungle safely. And as they were singing this song they began to paddle the canoes along homeward as hastily as they could, because "hastily, hastily, hastily the sun is going back to its place of yesterday" their ambition was to reach the town within a few minutes. The song which they were singing along went thus—

> *"Bulla—bul—laha: Shaka—bul—laha*
> *With all chocolates: bullaha—bul—laha*
> *Ice-cream: You scream: row o: row o o: row o o o*
> *Bulla—bul—laha: Shaka—bul—lah*
> *killed all the pigmies!*
> *Monday—Tuesday—with all Ice-cream:*
> *for Ice-cream: row o: row o o: row o o o . . ."*

As these cheerful men were paddling the canoes along the river it was so they were singing this song repeatedly and they were shouting with great joy whenever they remembered that they had already freed from the pigmies. Whenever we met another canoes on this river they would throw a lot of these fruits to the people who were inside them with joy. And this "reflecting eyes" were helping us too much whenever it was dark because it was so reflecting on the water that we did not miss our way till we reached my town after the sixth day that we were on the river.

Before we reached my town news had reached there that I had killed all the pigmies and that I was bringing a lot of hunters who had been detained by the pigmies, back to the town. And we hardly landed our canoes when the people ran to the canoes and embraced us with great joy.

Everyone was taken home by his family and my own family took my four brothers and I to the house as well. The following morning, a great merriment was performed throughout the town for our arrival.

After a few days I sold all the precious metals and I became a rich lady at once.

And that was the end of ADEBISI's adventure of the Jungle of the Pigmies. Adebisi was one of the brave huntswomen of those days gone by. Those women of those days had endured great dangers as well as the men of those days had endured great dangers.